Contents

100 JOLTS

Shockingly Short Stories

Michael A. Arnzen

100 JOLTS: Shockingly Short Stories © 2004 by Michael A. Arnzen
All rights reserved

Published by Raw Dog Screaming Press
Hyattsville, MD

First printing 2004

Editor: Vincent W. Sakowski
Cover image: Matt Sesow
Book design: Jennifer Barnes

Printed in the United States of America

ISBN 0-9745031-2-6

Library of Congress Control Number: 2003099176

www.rawdogscreaming.com

DEDICATION

TO
MY STUDENTS
& MY TEACHERS

&

FOR
BYRON ORLOCK
& GRIFFIN MILL

Appendices

Minimalist Horror

Boo! Eek! Ahhhh!

Horror is the genre of the one syllable word, the exclamation point, the elongated scream.

Notwithstanding the commercially successful novels of writers like Dickens and King, horror is predominantly a genre of the short story. Notably, both those popular writers mastered short forms first. But before them, Poe—credited with both the invention of the short story as a genre and being a founding father of today's horrific tale—predicated his work on the notion of the "single desired effect." That effect, in "The Cask of Amontillado," is the terrifying notion of imprisonment, which he achieved in under 2500 words. One could read that short tale as an extended metaphor for the human condition; one could even draft a dissertation on the tale's allegory for the writer's relationship to his own addiction. But the entertainment value is what mattered to him most—the emotional urgency. Poe was going for the *frisson* at the end. The chill. The shock. The surprising revelation of a secret plan, which the character of Fortunato (and the reader) only gets to glimpse momentarily before it is all too late.

Horror is the genre of the jolt, the shock, the spark. The horror story's conflict is always a matter of life and death, but death—even to an undead creature—always comes as a surprise. The climax of a horror tale is almost unilaterally a killing blow, catching someone or something unaware. Death almost always comes too soon—that's why we fear it. Life is always too short. Never long enough.

Horror's shortest stories replicate this logic, capturing the brevity of life in its most distilled form. Whether in the deeply felt *frisson* or the immediate spring of a surprise, horror requires brevity.

Less is more. And less is less.

A cold hand on the shoulder. A sharp bite on the neck. A rusty knife in the ribs.

Horror novels and films rely often on suspense—on holding one's breath as if that could extend life. Although it borrows heavily from the mystery and detective genre, horror is not a whodunit. Horror's mysteries are usually universally repressed truths, whereas suspense is a piano chord that can only be played so long. Horror bangs on the same piano as suspense, but it produces more chaotic chords. Cacophony, sometimes. Horror pounds the keys of the literary piano in staccato rhythm. Horror resides in the chirp of the *Psycho* soundtrack. The arc of Mother's knife. And the pulse-racing dribble and twist of the camera down the drain afterwards.

Horror is a thrill ride that's over before you expect to be, yet none too soon. If you stay aboard the ride for too long, you become immune to the curves that toss you around in your car. You see the cardboard cutouts coming. You might even stare at the safety mechanics with bemusement. Good horror is the shortest and most dangerous ride at the literary carnival. It doesn't give you the opportunity to study its architecture unless you ride it repeatedly.

Good dark poetry can capture the spirit of horror, too, in all its brevity and bravura. Baudelaire knew this. He also knew that that boundary-blurring form—the prose poem—could evoke the uncanny and the fantastic by bridging together the magic of poetic language with the belief inherent to narrative logic. Short, poetic horror combines the metonymy of madness with the metaphor of malignancy.

Horror is the most subversively experimental popular genre of them all. Sometimes it's a wolf in sheep's clothing on the mainstream paperback or video racks; sometimes it's an underground or occult treasure, a cult classic known only to a few. But it always offers a counterpoint to the moral *status quo* and the culture of boredom and repetition—it seeks to disrupt normalcy, to break boundary lines, to challenge the rules. It defamiliarizes, like all good literature should. Some call it childish, because of Halloween or YA monsters, but it appeals to teens only because it rebels against a culture that would over-protectively parent its people. Yet horror is not pop music; it is alternative rock on the literary radio. A space for emergent forms.

A trap door drops open. A jack springs out of its box, bearing a knife. Here's Johnny!

Horror readers expect the unexpected. The genre *in toto* therefore flaunts its literary experiment as a struggle to say something new when the reader least expects it. Minimalist horror fiction and short scary poems are not signs of a "short attention span" culture—instead, they are thought experiments that challenge the genre's more popular mainstream (and predictable) forms. They run counter to the mass marketed horror novels and two hour teen angst dramas. They present a snapshot of terror that fixes life and death perpetually in a brief moment of time, as formally structured and composed as the works of German Expressionism. Their brevity also prevents readers from spending time analyzing the monsters of horror long enough to spot the zipper running down their back.

Minimalist horror is a shotgun shell: a tightly wadded package of shrapnel designed for maximum coverage, minimal escape.

Boom. Hack. Slash.

It's bleeding that takes time. Not the injury that causes it. Bleeding is what you do afterward, reeling from the attack.

And the genre is renewed. The rebirth of the genre is always already a part of its death. Horror remains the genre of the undead.

Skull Fragments

Prologue: Diving in

One day, you take your daughter to the local fast food chain. She's only four, so after filling her belly full of milkshake, she jumps around in the corporate "Playland" they've got for hyperactive kiddies. Her favorite continent in Playland is the giant pen full of plastic balls which she loves to dive into and hide within, only to leap back out and scare other children whenever they enter the bin.

You eat a burger and it's business as usual, until you hear her scream. Authentically.

You turn, and for only a moment you think she's found some strange sort of puppet. But you quickly realize: your daughter holds a real human skull in her hands.

She vomits chocolate ice cream and french fries all over the multi-colored balls that surround her. She drops the skull and flails, struggling to get to you, as if she were drowning in plastic.

The skull bobs menacingly behind her head all the while until you rescue her and run to the counter for help.

No one in the building stops eating, not even after the police arrive and hold them for questioning. The restaurant manager sweats when they grill him, but otherwise just seems confused.

You and your daughter are interrogated thoroughly at the scene, given a business card with a badge on it, and told to avoid any reporters and be available for a follow-up conversation. You leave the restaurant, wondering about that skull—how small it was—how tiny. How similar in size to your daughter's head.

On the news that night, you learn that what your daughter had stumbled upon was just the beginning of a much more disturbing nightmare. All totaled, thirteen human skulls were discovered in the playpen. Each skull was boiled and bleached clean. They discovered that each skull had writing on it: enigmas finely etched on various plates and areas of the bony mass, strange tales inscribed with impeccable penmanship in black indelible ink.

You are for the first time thankful that your daughter is not old enough to read. In your dreams that night, you swim in a multi-colored ocean of billiard balls, diving for skulls. Each descent immerses you in a painful, porcelain coldness. Fingering blindly, you handle the skulls and bring each to the surface, removing your goggles and mouthpiece before reading its story. Some are spelled out on the forehead like a tattoo. Others require cracking open like some absurd fortune cookie to get to the truths they hide. And all of them seem to be printed in your own handwriting...

1. Gardener

I hated every single word he ever spoke. So I clipped his spinal cord and turned him into a vegetable. But I forgot to water him. When he rotted, I pruned his skull, removing the jaw. Then I turned him upside down and grew tomatoes in his potted head.

2. Skull Scraper

Finishing the skull job is like scraping ice from a windshield: I want nothing left of him when I don his bone mask. But the deep curves resist my razor, his meat clinging to the sinew as if—finally knowing the life in death—he wants to see what I see.

3. Gastronomy

The intellectual zombie knows not to go directly for the brains. Understanding physics, he fears fire not. He burns his victim civilly, upright in a metal chair. At boiling point, he steeps a fleshy teabag in the skull, concocting a fine aperitif of herbal cranial fluid before his dinner roast.

4. Soft Spots

During his trial, the baby killer confessed when the lawyer produced his claw hammer. He said he was only collecting their soft spots. The place he kept them? In his heart, obviously. This appeal to pity did not work on the jury. Years later, in the confinement of his cell, he died of a "heart attack." The prisoners all agreed that he'd cried in the night like a thousand baby girls.

5. Tapping Charley

Tandy always marvels at the soft dime-sized scar on the front of Charley's forehead, popping out like a belly button on his temple. Charley calls it his third eye. He swears it's not a birthmark, but a scar from a suicidally risky attempt at trepanation.

Ten years ago, drunk in Katmandu, he tried self-trepanation, armed only with a nail gun, a brown bottle of H_2O_2, a silk handkerchief and a pint of Chinese Rice Vodka. He can't remember how it worked, exactly, or how he managed to survive the messy process, but he knows the tap in his skull relieved him of a lifetime of stress. He was so relaxed afterward, they even had to kick him out of the Marines— he'd gone too soft, they'd said. Too mellow for maneuvers.

Now he hands Tandy an awl, but his wife refuses to pick the scab, even if it means he'll stop beating her, like he keeps promising. She doesn't want to poke his hardened over crust of an eye. Instead, she goes for one of his two good ones.

6. The Ugly Thing

The ugly thing about a cat licking a man's exposed bloody brain isn't the way the lobes stick to the furry tongue; it's the way the brain wobbles after the tongue lets go. Quivering in its bonebowl of clear fluid as if it were alive. Quivering as if the tongue had tickled it. Quivering as if brains ever quivered inside the skull in the first place.

7. The Bitter Wife

First she boils it. Then she cracks apart the primary pieces. She polishes each bone slab as smooth as a pearled plate. Then she continues their fight where it left off, shattering these new dishes on the floor.

8. The Strangest Skull

The archaeologist had brushed his share of dust from buried bones in sand dunes. But he'd never seen anything like Buktakamun VI—the infamous "blind pharaoh" of Niveah. Bukta VI's skeletal remains were all normal, save for the skull. His cranium had no fissures. And there were plates of bone where his eye sockets should have been.

A thorough investigation disclosed that the cause of Bukta's death was a blow to the back of the head with a hammer. The archaeologist knew of the legend of the blind pharaoh whose eyes shone light as bright as the sun, but dared not speak it to his colleagues. Who would believe that his head had been opened like a piggy bank, by some impatient seeker of truth? No—the archaeologist would keep silent, holding his secret locked as tight inside as the light that once broiled within the pharaoh's head. Some truths are meant to be kept locked in the crypt.

9. Resonant Eyes

If you lick your fingertip and run it steadily around the rim of the eye socket, you can produce a tone as deep and hollow as a bassoon. Perhaps even better. But more uncanny is the aura of color that projects into the dark hole of the socket if you continue to play the head instrument—a hazy marble of light that mimics the dead man's original eye color. But you won't have the courage to spin that rim and stare at that ghost eye for too long, because the song it sings begins to sound more and more like an alien language, murmuring your name.

10. Fissures

Do they hold the bones together or do they threaten to break it apart? If the skull holds the brain in place, what holds the skull? The man with the scalpel moves toward the tied-up surgeon's face, probing for answers.

11. Knock Off the Auction Block

When the package arrived I tore it open. The human skull was in the hatbox, packed in bubble wrap just like the eBay listing said it would be. I slid it out and held it before me like a kid who got a football helmet for Christmas. It was bigger and heavier than I expected. And whiter. Bleached white. The listing online said it was authentic, but I didn't expect it to be as white as an eggshell. I'd read that the serial killer enjoyed cooking some of the body parts he'd eaten, but I'd never heard that he'd actually boiled a human head. And as time passed and the skull sat under the glass of my trophy case, staring back at me, I wondered more and more whether I'd really invested in the killer's fine handiwork or just blew my money on someone's old garbage.

12. Doofus

A boy tears the jaw off his brother's skull. "Who's the doofus now?" he asks, as if expecting the grim overbite to answer.

Epilogue: Up For Air

The final skull, wet in your hands, is your daughter's. And she certainly has stories to tell.

Limber

It started with his left pinkie. A plunking sound, the fraying of rope, then the release of tiny bones from one another to tumble down and swish all loose inside his finger like pebbles in a shoe. After that came the rest of his fingers, one by one—*plunk, plunk, plunk, ka-plunk.* Jimmy shook his hand the way a nurse shakes a thermometer and he felt the chunky material inside the floppy bag of skin swim around. It tickled, as though his hand had fallen asleep. The thin skin of his fingers was soft and when he held up his hand the five fingers fell over and behind his palm like those on an empty glove. The fingers strained pale on their meaty hinges.

Then—probably from all the messing around he was doing with his hand—down came the arm. And when those long hard pieces inside slid down past his elbow and into Jimmy's five-fingered bone sack, they gave him new, profound knuckles. Lumpy, monstrous tumescence bulged where the back of his wrist should have been. And the bulby knob of his humerus bloated up his palm as if he'd developed a gigantic boil. Cords and muscles slathered around in the bone stew like stringy meat in a Chinese soup.

Free of their clingy limbs, his shoulders were exceptionally loose. Jimmy imagined that this was the ultimate goal of any back rub or visit to the chiropractor: to truly liberate the limbs. He'd lost complete use of his hands, true, but he felt fantastic.

And then his skull dropped down hard into the holster of his clavicle and his lungs sloughed off the coat rack of his ribs and his spine twanged like a spring released from tension. Jimmy fell to his shins, then fell right into them as gravity sunk his innards straight down inside the bag of his body. Bones that had never met before encountered each other with a loud knock and thud as the pile of parts on the floor rose up around him.

Truly stress free, Jimmy would have smiled if he was still attached to his mouth. Instead he relaxed. Eyeballs were all that embodied him. One pointed to the left and the other pointed to the right and he marveled over how wonderful it was to be able to see in two opposing directions while he waited for the dog to discover him.

And then the lenses slipped down from their orbits like bad contacts sliding on the cornea. And then the whole world seemed just as soupy and limber as he.

OBICTIONARY
(for Edward Gorey)

Alma almost got away. Bailey was blasted bloody into the blacktop. Christa, conked unconscious. Dora, gored. Eddie bled as dry as Freddy. Gordon's goopy on the ground. Heather, weathered in chains on the rainy rooftop. Indigo, spinned to and fro in the ceiling fan. Jack, put in the box. Kyle killed. Louis juiced. Mike microwaved. Ned needs a head. Oscar is nothing but scar tissue now. Peter Peter, pumpkin eater, puked up his poisoned pie. Queenie wears her tiara upside-down, the jewels all jabbed into her temples. Rusty congeals in a net of iron chains in the shallow end of a brown pool. Saran Wrap muffles Sara's screams. Tom's now tomato juice. Vince, minced and forked into fondue. Wayne wanes, dribbling the rest of his life into a boring basin. X marks the spot where Mark was spotted in my crosshairs. Yolanda won't yodel without a throat. And Zorro won't zee tomorrow.

And who could forget you? You will get yours, unusually, soon.

Degrees of Separation

Something bubbles in the hot Jacuzzi. Glen sheepishly apologizes and Sally giggles at his joke. They stew in their juices for awhile, slowly edging closer to one another as though carried on the carpet of foam air-jetting beneath them. Another two bubbles burp up, and Sally titters and blushes, making goo-goo eyes at Glen, but Glen is frowning and beginning to sweat. He puts an arm around her now, and their bodies slip-slide together, somehow cooler than the water, but they both avoid one another's eyes and stare over at the opposite end of the tub, waiting for proof. Another series of bubbles blurt up on the surface there. What the hell *was* that, Glen signals with his eyes as he fondles Sally's strap, but Sally is laughing maniacally now as the frothy water finally reaches a boil.

PUNISHMENT

Exhausted, Mother rocks in the shadows of Child's bedroom, realizing that her storytelling has finally performed its magic. A snore of adult proportions pours out from somewhere inside Child's big soft head. Mother sees Child's plastic baby doll on the floor and picks it up. The plastic skull is collapsed and dented, like a flat basketball that's gently been stepped upon. It should have been tucked away, Mother muses. The doll is missing an arm; the remaining appendage pinwheels loosely in a neglected socket. An eyelid swims melancholic, floating somewhere between open and shut as Mother props the doll on her lap. Child stirs in the bed, rolling onto her good side. Mother violently squeezes a spongy leg. The doll's eyes flutter open. Child screams.

Nightmare Job #1

When skull strikes wood, the screaming stops. You hear it thump three more times. By the time you turn the corner, you see the supervisor clutching a cat by the tail, swinging the animal down with his arm like a man wielding a mallet, beating the brains out on the tabletop. Some yellow matter spurts out its ear and lands in a gob by your feet as if the dead feline had sneezed. Its eyes dangle in blackened sockets, looking incredibly large to you.

"Come here, newbie," the punisher says with a sneer. "I'll show you how we do it around here."

You cinch up your green lawn and garden smock, adjust your name badge, and approach the table strewn with entrails and gore.

The gardener tosses the carcass into the drum that reads "Blood Meal" and reaches into the mewling kitten cage with his massively gloved hand.

You roll up your sleeves and get to work.

Turn of the Season

She tried to cheer me up by saying everything grows again in the spring. Look at the grass and the trees. Nature thrives in the spring. But I couldn't stop looking at her. And the dark shadows etched permanently into her marbled features. When I finally looked at the grass beneath my feet—a rectangular plot a different shade than the rest—I realized she was right. The sod really was thriving, sprouting green shoots among her freshly turned soil. Someone was cheering up now. Maybe her.

Pop-Up Killer

I'm very protective of my privacy on the web. I have all the best protection software on the market: firewalls, Trojan horse detectors, cookie blockers, ad killers, and surf history purgers. When I reboot my system, it loads up like a computer in a day care center: it's that clean.

So you can imagine my surprise when an ad popped up out of nowhere one day while I was researching notation for organ music: *CLICK HERE TO KILL GOD NOW!* it blinked in ugly yellow and red, like some animated detergent box.

Naturally, I was furious. My pop-up popper wasn't working properly. Either I needed to upgrade, or the capitalist bastards had once again figured out a way to outsmart the latest technology. I throttled my mouse and moved to click on the big X in the upper right corner of the dialogue box to close the offending window.

But I left-clicked too soon.

I expected to be taken to some sham site that was selling books or videos or who knows what.

Instead, the world *around* the computer loaded a new page.

And my chair came to life beneath me.

Madly, I clicked and prayed. Then Satan's head suddenly popped up from behind the monitor and shook an oily, fanged finger at me that said, *tsk-tsk, too late,* as the organs of a million new visitors began to browse me.

Brain Candy

He was a goner. So I shot him in the face and his head burst like a flesh piñata, spraying the zombie kiddies with its brain candy. This slowed them all down as they raked inside the emptied husk of fruit on its shoulders. Then they tore at one another for the morsels on one another's shirtsleeves and collars. The whole sick scene almost looked like a birthday party from my distance. I took my time picking them off, one by one, from the rooftop.

WHITE OUT

Everyone went white.

I don't know exactly when it happened—sometime in the middle of my everyday life—perhaps when I entered and exited an elevator. Whatever the time might have been, the origin was hidden from me. What I saw was unbelievable, yet it was verified by every face and form I encountered: humanity had gone albino.

On my office floor, albino secretaries were pepper-dusted with toner. White-skinned clerks chatted on the phone in their cubicles, the veins pink on their chins and elbows. At lunch, I saw albinos eating hotdogs at a food stand, the pink meat disappearing into their pink mouths and teeth more yellow than their skin. In the park, albinos sat on benches like fine china statues, feeding the birds with stiff gestures. I found myself drifting around the city, popping into buildings here and there, staring in wonder at the albinos everywhere. Albinos kissing, obscenely mashing red colored tongues between their mouths. Albinos sporting green and blue make up. Albinos wearing Ray Bans like something out of *Star Trek*. They seemed unaware of their difference.

At one point, I ran to the nearest public restroom, where a tall albino in a business suit was streaming an arc of banana-yellow urine into a porcelain urinal that seemed obscenely white between the man's leg. He avoided eye contact more than men usually do at urinals. I seized the mirrors and stared at my complexion: same mildly tanned face, same sunburned trucker's arm from the daily cab ride, same blue and white eyes.

The albino in the bathroom was gone by the time I turned to ask him if he knew what had bleached the world. A trail of yellow droplets ran out the door as if he'd run away in a hurry.

I tried to follow, but he was gone.

I tried to get a cab, but no one would pull over.

Whites were everywhere. I couldn't avoid them. Something inside of me wanted to slash them, to see their blood spill red and confirm their humanity.

Isolated, yet surrounded, I ran toward my apartment complex on the other side of the city.

I feared discrimination, of course. I thought they'd turn on me. Their eyes were webbed with pink veins, throbbing with fear and distrust. I was the inhuman one.

They were waiting at my building. I noticed a gang of them, dressed in pink business suits, milling about the hallway to my apartment like pale, well-dressed skinheads, colluding before an attack. They surrounded me in the elevator and—*en masse*—quietly ushered me to the parking garage below the building. They shoved me into a car and placed a hood over my head. They drove me for hours.

I thought they were taking me somewhere secret to murder me. Instead, they wanted to steal me away from public view. I was an oddity to them. An aberration. In need of protection.

They put me on display. They tossed me meat, but I felt more like a lobster in a seafood restaurant tank than a caged lion. Tourists would come and gawk, the pinks of their eyes jittering wetly with need.

"You remind us," one once said, "of the beauty of blood." And behind him, I saw a pale man tear open the neck of a cat and brutally dine.

Stabbing for Dummies

REMEMBER: Always grasp the knife by the end that is rubbery, leathery, or otherwise soft to the touch. If you don't, you'll find it very difficult to dial for an ambulance.

1. Stabbing has an objective. It is easy to forget this. Don't. Especially when it gets messy.

2. Cutting is drawing a line. Sticking is poking a hole. There is a difference.

WARNING: Blood may spurt, gout, or spray in very unexpected ways. Always wear goggles and gloves when stabbing. Or perhaps a plastic mask. It not only protects, but also provides a dramatic effect that makes up for the messiness.

3. Show your victim the blade before you use it. Take your time on this step. Especially if wearing a mask.

4. If you must be sneaky, then consider "the approach" to your target as a skill, much like hunting. You can sidle up to your victim and surprise them from behind, the blade biting skin like a tongue in a kiss. Or you can hug them and then tickle their ribs with the tip. Or— if they have no means of chopping off your arms—you can just lunge. (Although it wins cool points, it is considered bad form to throw a blade from a distance if your target does not see it coming…this is the equivalent of stabbing your victim in the back. Unless, of course, you throw like a girl. Then it's just embarrassing! Practice, practice, practice, no matter what your gender.)

SHORTCUT: Knowledge of the circulatory system can save time.

5. Always let the blade do the bulk of the work. Do not twist, saw or chop. Simply slide.

REMEMBER: Always sharpen your blade before the hunt, unless you want jagged cuts. Sharp cuts looks cooler, but ragged cuts hurt more. It all comes down to your goals (see Chapter Three).

6. Do not flinch if your victim raises his arms to shield or even clutch at you. Trust in your blade.

TIP: Pretend you're painting. This not only makes your work more effective, it's fun! (Remember Zorro? Emulate the man. But keep it simple. You're not writing your name in the snow, as it were. Simple and bold is best: one letter, symbol, Satanic or otherwise. Remember: Zorro did it with a 'Z', not with "Z-O-R-R-O.")

7. If you look your victim in the eye, you will find yourself filled with an overwhelming desire to stab them again and again until they look away. They will not. Their gaze will simply intensify. Unless you stab them in the eyes or the groin. Give your victim something to think about.

REMEMBER: Flesh is flesh…is flesh. Knives do not discriminate. However, you should avoid bony areas which may chip or otherwise dull your blade.

8. Blades leave traces behind them. A serration pattern leaves foot-prints in the flesh and can lead to your arrest. A fleck of metal that you leave in your wake can send you to the electric chair. Use carbide steel and be sure to sharpen the blade both before and after the stabbing in order to change the edge pattern. Also, nothing is worse than trying to stab someone with an inferior blade and having it break. So don't scrimp on the blade, but always remember to pay with cash—and never purchase from the same dealer twice.

TIP: Although you will be tempted, never use your victim's spit on your sharpening stone!

9. You may kiss your bloodied blade after a kill. Or, for that matter, lick

it in front of your victim before that final fatal stab. Don't worry about contracting disease. You earned it.

10. Conceal a backup blade somewhere on your person. This blade could help out if you find yourself in a defensive position.

TIP: Once you've mastered this process, try using two blades at the same time for an extra challenge! Two blades can also look twice as cool. And generally speaking, the bigger the blade the better. This is a case where size does matter.

11. Consider etching your favored blade with your signature or a motto. Or perhaps one of these directions. Or a suicide note.

(Written with Vincent W. Sakowski)

THE COW CAFE

Kyle has brought you out to The Cow Cafe for coffee. You did not want to come, but you say nothing. He says the coffee is the best around. And you love a good cup of joe.

It's two miles outside the city limits, in an area you rarely drive, where farms still harvest grain and raise animals. The Cafe is likely a former slaughterhouse. You can tell by the faded paint on the side of the weather-beaten wooden building: BUTCHERED MEATS. The tarred and faded brown wood reminds you of so many Westerns. Not coffee.

But you make your way past a surprising number of cars corralled in the lot and you head into the building by plunking up a wooden ramp and shoving the heavy front door open, feeling like an authentic cowboy. The place is noisy, even somewhat bohemian in its Western decor. Everything's wood and chrome and the dull din of patrons clumping across the floor fills your ears. Large paintings of cows munching grass encircle the room. They have squares cut into their hides, with daylight shining through. Each is like a surrealist piece by Magritte. The customers slurp their drinks while seated at what appear to be medical tables—large stainless steel surfaces with drainage holes and white butcher paper tablecloths. They remind you of doctor's offices and butcher shops.

There's a line at the coffee bar. Kyle examines his choices in a large menu that's written in fancy purple lettering overhead. You hear the grind of machines and the burp of foam and the tinkle of spoons everywhere. It's dawning on you just how popular this place is, despite its location. They must serve good coffee.

The menu is littered with invented names for drinks. You can't tell what's what, let alone how to pronounce half of them. They appear to be puns, mostly: Bovine Brew, Mooka Milka, and stuff like that. You decide to play it safe by ordering a simple house coffee.

Kyle says he can't make up his mind.

You finally get to the front of the line. A punk with spiky black hair, a bullring in his nose, and a leather apron asks what you'd like. You feign indecision as you look up at the menu one last time.

Then someone rudely elbows his way next to you. "I ordered a *Cafe au Lait*, dude. This has no cream at all in it."

The punk in the apron looks perturbed. His nose ring dangles menacingly when he sneers like Billy Idol. He takes the cup with him through some saloon doors behind the counter that apparently lead to the kitchen.

And when they swing open you see a young cow dangling from meat hooks. It twists its big wet brown eye at you and moos.

The saloon doors swing again and you see the punk put the *Cafe au Lait* under the bovine's belly.

They swing again and he's fumbling with a pink udder like a grotesque nipple. He's squirting milk right into the cup as the cow kicks from the pain of dangling.

You assume you're imagining this but the sound of mooing is unmistakable.

The punk returns and hands the complainer his drink. "There you are, *sir*." He says "sir" like a fifteen year old would: falsely. Then he turns to you, wiping white milk and blood from his hands on his leather apron. He sighs and rolls his eyes. "How can I help you?"

You're glad you're playing it safe. "Small house blend," you say, not even sure if you'll dare to drink it.

"Caf, half-caf or decaf?" the punk asks, ringing it up.

"Caffeinated, of course." You remember the cow. "And just sugar. No cream."

He nods with approval. He turns around and fills a cup with steaming black liquid from a nearby tankard. You relax. Then he heads toward the saloon doors.

"Wait, I said no milk..." you utter, but you can't get it all out before he pushes through and disappears into the back room.

You hear the familiar moo.

Followed by a bovine scream unlike any noise you've ever heard. It sounds more like a pig being pushed through a sausage grinder, live.

The punk pops his head out the door. A bloody cleaver drips in his grip. "Did you say calf or decalf?"

You almost correct him. But you hear the pun in your ears and it isn't funny and you run.

As you race along the tables, the clientele of the cafe watch you with a bemused expression that suggests that you aren't the first to have turned tail. You notice that a few are eating some very disturbing deserts. Men saw into cakes of chocolate-brown patties with overly large butcher's knives. Children appear to be suckling soft serve from bright pink udders, squishing the mess into their mouths like a chef squeezes a frosting tube. You think you hear Kyle order something called a "double clot-te" from somewhere behind you as you push your way through the door.

You want to run, but you're too far from town and since no one seems to be coming after you, and the sky is as blue as it always was, you decide to wait for him by the car and pull yourself together. Out behind the Cafe, cows masticate and eyeball you like you're crazy. You feel helpless, sitting on Kyle's hood.

Kyle drives you back to the city as though nothing's happened. You don't mention it. The next time he takes you out to lunch, he has the audacity to take you to a burger joint. You remind him that you're a vegetarian, but he never seems to learn.

HANDICAPPED SPOT

I'm driving my friend Paul to the airport to meet his girlfriend Tina, when he tells me that her plane lands in two minutes.

I speed up my minivan to the Short-Term Parking Lot entrance. A machine spits out a ticket like a cardboard tongue, and when I pull it out the gate lifts its robotic metal arm as lethargically as a volunteer.

The lot appears full but I shoot toward the row of cars closest to the airport's front entrance.

"You'll never find a spot there," Paul says, unslouching for a moment to scan over the sea of car rooftops as if to verify it. "Besides, they're all for compacts anyway." He slouches again and checks his watch.

I gun it over a speed bump and there's a loud crash when the tools under my seat and the junk in my glove box jump from the impact. I'm smiling because Paul hit his head on the ceiling of the van, matching the sound effect perfectly.

Paul deserved that. He's been rushing me the whole way to the airport—a three hour drive from our small town. The city traffic makes him nervous. And he hasn't seen Tina since her accident a year ago.

"How much time we got?"

"She lands in a minute and a half."

"Shit. I'll find a good place to park." I'm passing by the best spots—all of them are filled with compacts, as Paul predicted, but there are a few choice locations right by the front entrance. I slow down.

"You can't park there. They're all handicapped."

"So what? We're late. Isn't that a handicap?"

"Very funny." Paul leers at me, ready to argue. Then I remember that his girl, Tina, is missing her left forearm.

I step on the brake anyway. "Maybe I can drop you off here," I suggest, "and hook up with you later."

Paul's brow drops down heavy. Tina is not only missing a forearm.

She's got a hook in place of her hand.

"I need you to help me carry the bags." He starts shaking his leg nervously and the car seat squeaks.

I hate that.

I gun the van again and zip toward another speed bump. He sees it coming and braces for the impact.

My tools and glove box junk rattle and crash.

"What the hell is all that? Sounds like your engine's ready to fall out."

"There's a spot opening up!" I see a pair of red brake lights—a telltale sign of someone starting their engines—on an Audi two rows away from the front entrance. I pull up to the zone and turn on my blinkers, telling the world that I call this spot.

But then a guy gets out of the Audi and locks the door. He carries a bag and smirks when he passes us, shaking his head at me as if I was the village idiot.

I hate that. I gun the car and return to circling the lot.

Paul's leg starts shaking again, like a horny monkey's.

I really hate that.

I reach for the toolbox under my seat.

"I don't see anyplace to park anywhere. You don't think they'd let us in this lot if they were all out of spots, do you?"

"There's only x number of spots. Maybe the gate thinks I'm handicapped…"

"Nah, couldn't be." Paul's second leg joins his first—they shudder symmetrically as he examines his watch.

"…when really, you're the one who's differently-abled." I swing the hammer at his head. He's knocked cold but that damned leg's still kicking. I pull over and line up my saw on the nearest thigh. And I move fast. I don't want to lose any of those spots.

TAKE OUT

She lunged at me with the pizza cutter, slashing the wafer-thin disk across my chest and press-rolling it so fast she must have cut at least six slices out of me. My nipples crimped below the blade like pepperoni, but I'm not round like a pie. Instead, my limbs fell off, spilling their contents like poorly stuffed crust. And she wasn't happy with my toppings. So she loaded me up with her own and tossed my shell into her oven. The garlic and peppers stung worse than my boiling sauce and melting meat. After the broil, I waned on her rack. She put me in a box, rather than in her mouth. She let me dribble and drain all greasy in cardboard. It was then that I realized she liked her men cold and leftover. I congealed and apologized, but that didn't stop her from delivering me to you.

A CHANGE IN POLICY

A dull knock upon the thick oak door. Whispers of sloshing red blood and yellow viscera in a stained white bucket. An impatient toe tap.

"Come in."

The short man rubs a wet, rubber-gloved hand down the side of his white lab coat, leaving a smear of gore trailing down his jacket before turning the doorknob and stepping inside.

"Boss," the nervous little man states with a thin thread of determination. "I've come as spokesman for the rest of the employees. We just don't like this disgusting work, and we won't have it anymore. You've turned this place into a slaughterhouse!"

Behind the large desk scattered with computer listings of names and addresses, the boss leans back in his chair. He slowly raises a hand to his white beard and strokes its nappy fur, feigning deep thought and concentration. He smiles a thick-cheeked smile. The worker nervously watches, waiting for the boss' reaction.

Finally the boss' voice erupts from beneath his hairy chin, sounding oddly jocular despite its serious tone: "I told you and the rest of the workers that there's been a change in policy and that's that. I want blood and guts, and that's what I'm gonna get...even if I have to fire the whole lot of you!" The boss smiles again, but his chubby cheeks redden in restrained fury.

"But it goes against our purpose, Chief!"

The big man impatiently groans. "Do I have to explain it to you again? The world has changed and it's time for us to change along with it. It's a sick world, and by gum, we're gonna fight fire with fire!"

"But the coal industry has always worked so well..."

"I said that I want guts...now go get me guts!"

"You want guts? Here, have your guts!" The worker upturns the bucket across the boss' desk, drenching the tabletop with foamy red gore. Intestines slap and slither through the ocean of splatter, sliming across the desk like water snakes.

The boss fishes a long computer sheet out from beneath the sea of entrails and plasma. He holds the paper up in the air and shakes it, a frown overtaking his previously jolly face. "Aw, look what you did! You ruined it!" The boss throws the list of addresses at the employee, cursing. "Now how the hell am I going to know who's been naughty and nice?"

The worker audibly gulps.

The boss stands up, pulling a buck knife from the pocket of his over-sized red pants. "Guess I'm gonna have to stuff everyone's stocking with the new product now!" The boss jacks open the shiny blade. "And you, my humble employee, owe me exactly one bucket of guts."

The boss lunges with a jingle.

PARTNERS

You are uncertain about your new partner.

He's whipped. He keeps looking over his shoulder, as if expecting his wife to give her approval. But she's not in the room. "We decided when we married that we would collaborate on everything," he says, wiping his brow. "Our partnership was bound as tight as Siamese twins joined at the skull. We split all meals and even shared forks to save on washing dishes. We shared pillows and pills. We're virtually the same person."

I understand completely, you reply. And you do.

He pulls at his beard and muses. "You can't fathom how hard it is for me to sign this particular contract!"

Yes, I can, you say, handing him the steaming hot pen. Then you tell him with your blood red eyes alone that your bond is just as close, and truly—truly—eternal. Your barbed tail curls somewhere on the floor beneath you, looping his foot.

He signs her name as well.

Mustachio Moon

On the midnight of the full moon, I looked up in the sky and noticed that the man in the moon had grown a mustache. At first I was not bothered by this quirky observation. It seemed sort of cute. But later that night I could not sleep peacefully because the very thought began to disturb me. What would cause the moon to change so radically overnight? At work the next day, I asked if anyone else had noticed the upper lip of the moon, but my coworkers just laughed and waved my crazy notions away as they bustled about their business.

A full cycle passed as I waited in anticipation of the next full moon. When it rose, I was amazed to notice that the man in the moon now had a full beard! I woke up my wife and children and made them look up to the night sky to confirm my vision. Everyone saw it. My wife said we all must be dreaming. My oldest son said it looked like a terrorist. My youngest daughter was horrified and ran crying into her room. The middle child said she saw Grandpa in the sky...no, Santa. My wife and I laughed. We noted more than just the beard—its eyes and nose, too seemed more prominent by contrast. Together we held hands and watched the big bearded moon until we fell asleep.

The next day, I checked the newspapers and the television. No one had reported about the hirsute moon! I was amazed by my coworkers' audacity when they all laughed at my observations again. But this time I knew they were the crazy ones. Was the whole world blind? Was everyone loony? Next time I would make sure they all looked up to the sky at midnight. I researched the astronomical charts, I marked my calendar, and I wrote letters to not only all of my coworkers but also all of the news stations and papers and magazines, even all of the government officials all over the planet. I urged them to look to the heavens on the next full moon.

On the day of its arrival, my family sat in our backyard and watched. My whole neighborhood was out, staring at the sky. I knew my letter campaign had worked. At midnight, the moon came out with its full beard and mustache. And even more hair had grown on its round cheeks and shiny head. Vindicated, I shouted to the world: "Look! I am not crazy! See! The man in the moon really does have facial hair!"

And then it smiled down upon me. Wide. The werewolf moon bore its sharp fangs.

The mouth moved closer—got larger and larger—and I suddenly thought: *This is it. The Earth is full. Far too full.*

RETURN OF THE
LIVING DEAD

Finally, I poke a hole through the graveyard soil that has imprisoned me for eons. A rod of warm light pierces the darkness. I reach for freedom, but my pseudopod lands on a boulder of gravel that twists and pulls free in the soil. I clutch and tumble, cursing the eternal gravity of the grave.

Who Wants to be a Killionaire?

MERIDEATH: How will you get out of this one? Is it:
A. Eat your wrists off below the shackles.
B. Bite down, choke on your tongue, and drown in your own blood.
C. Hold your breath forever.
D. Starve.

IAN: Ooo. I know this one. I know it. Could be A. Could be C. I know it's not D. That's too easy.

[IAN nibbles a finger.] Umm...

MERIDEATH: You can only choose one, Ian. And 'Um' is not a letter. [Canned laughter]

IAN: Umm...it's not B.

MERIDEATH: [Leaning forward.] Are you sure?

IAN: Well. Sort of. I mean, if I bit off my tongue, I wouldn't be able to answer the question. Would I?

MERIDEATH: [Grimaces.]

IAN: I might still be able to use hand signals...

MERIDEATH: [Frowns.]

IAN: ...which I couldn't do if I chose A. Oh god, this is so hard!

MERIDEATH: That's the idea.

IAN: [IAN's head lolls from one shoulder to the other as he lethargically mulls over his options.]

MERIDEATH: Ian, you appear to be wavering.

IAN: I'm dizzy.

MERIDEATH: May I remind you that you've still got all of your Death-Lines left?

IAN: I do?

MERIDEATH: Yes, Ian. Would you like to use one of your DeathLines?

IAN: I do. I think.

MERIDEATH: You can Mask-the-Audience, use your Fifty-Fifty. Or…

IAN: I want to Debone-a-Friend.

MERIDEATH: Debone-a-Friend. Are you sure, Ian?

IAN: I'm definite.

MERIDEATH: All right. Who are we going to Debone?

IAN: Marty.

MERIDEATH: Why Marty?

IAN: He's a professional contortionist.

MERIDEATH: Good choice. [MERIDEATH rolls her eyes and the audience laughs.] Okay, we're dialing Marty thanks to our good friends at Slay T & T.

IAN: [Taps his foot and idly looks down at the chains that slide around on the well-polished marble floor with every tap.]

MERIDEATH: [Opens the chamber on her revolver and idly counts bullets.]

IAN: Why isn't he answering?

MERIDEATH: [Snapping the gun shut with a sharp flick of the wrist.] Maybe he knows that we're calling.

MARTY: Hello?

MERIDEATH: Is this Marty?

MARTY: Yes, it is. Who's there?

MERIDEATH: Marty, this is Merideath Vieerie from *Killionaire*.

MARTY: Merry who? I thought Greenjizz was supposed to call.

MERIDEATH: Greenge is no longer with us. Heart trouble. So how are you this evening?

MARTY: To tell you the truth, Merideath, I'm in a lot of pain. The morphine your guys are using isn't good enough.

MERIDEATH: [Laughs.] All right. We have your friend Ian on the line and he's kind of in a pickle.

MARTY: So am I. Thanks a helluva lot, Ian.

IAN: Don't blame me! They made me choo…

MARTY: Oh, I guess having my humerus removed will help me on the job. But still…

MERIDEATH: Now, now. The clock is already ticking, Ian. Twenty-five seconds.

IAN: Okay, okay. Marty. Here's the question. How will you get out of this one? A) Eat your wrists off, B) Choke on your tongue, C) Asphyxiate, or D) Starve.

MARTY: You've gotta be kidding.

IAN: Help me, Marty! I don't know the answer!

MERIDEATH: Fifteen seconds.

MARTY: You think I know? My right arm is boneless chuck. And— oh no. NO!

IAN: [Softly.] Marty?

MARTY: Please, not the other arm! Please! [Wailing.]

MERIDEATH: Ten seconds.

IAN: Oh god. Marty?

MARTY: Just kill me. Kill me now.

IAN: Marty! We're running out of time!

MARTY: Gahgle. [We hear snaps and splinters and meaty twisting.]

IAN: Just try, Marty. Try! Maybe if you answer the question they'll stop…

MARTY: More morphine? Yer so sweet.

MERIDEATH: Five seconds.

IAN: Marty!

MARTY: Uhn-hun. What was D again?

IAN: D) Starve.

MARTY: I do wanna starve. Please?

IAN: Are you sure?

MARTY: Anythins bedder dan dis. I thing.

IAN: You think?

MARTY: Skudgle warbo dulsigahn.

MERIDEATH: I'm afraid…[buzzer sound interrupts]…Time's up.

IAN: Oh no.

MERIDEATH: So what's it going to be, Ian?

IAN: Marty thinks it's D. I thought there was no way in hell it was D.

MERIDEATH: I believe Marty was wishful thinking.

IAN: You do? Well, if that's the case…

MERIDEATH: Was.

IAN: Now you don't?

MERIDEATH: No, now *he* doesn't.

IAN: Huh?

MERIDEATH: Look, what I think doesn't matter. Do you trust your old friend Marty or do you go with your gut?

IAN: I don't know. Starving just seems wrong to me.

MERIDEATH: There are other options.

IAN: [Whimpering.] There are?

MERIDEATH: You've got two Deathlines left.

IAN: That's right! And I'm still uncertain about A or C. C. A. CA. Cah. Ca-ca.

MERIDEATH: [Aiming the gun.] Ian. Focus.

IAN: Right.

MERIDEATH: What's it going to be? Would you like to Mask-the-Audience or use your Fifty-Fifty?

IAN: Fifty-Fifty might work.

MERIDEATH: Okay. We're going to eliminate two of the family members you brought with you today, leaving only two relatives left, one of which will be allowed to give you advice.

IAN: What?! That wasn't in the rulebook!

MERIDEATH: [Raises her pistol in IAN's direction. IAN braces and cringes. MERIDEATH aims over IAN's shoulder and fires.]

IAN: [He opens his eyes in disbelief.] Mom!

MERIDEATH: [Fires again.]

IAN: [Strains his neck, trying to peer over his shoulder.]

MERIDEATH: Judges?

IAN: If I ever get out of here, I'll kill you Merideath.

MERIDEATH: Well what do you know? I didn't hit her. Your mother's still with us. Along with your little sister. And since you've already shouted her name, let's go to the video and see what she thinks. Mrs. T?

IAN'S MOM: Oh my.

MERIDEATH: Mrs. T, your son is in a pickle. Please respond.

IAN'S MOM: Oh my god.

MERIDEATH: [Reloading.] Mrs. T., I have to ask you to focus on the matter at hand. What advice do you have for your son regarding this question?

IAN'S MOM: Oh my god...MY GOD! IAN, RUN FOR YOUR LIFE! IT'S RIGGED!

MERIDEATH: Heh-heh. Mrs. T, I'm afraid running is not one of the answers.

IAN: Quit badgering her, Merideath!

IAN'S MOM: Ahhh!

MERIDEATH: Mrs. T, do you have an answer for us?

IAN'S MOM: Ayeeeeee!

IAN: What are you people DOING to her?

MERIDEATH: Mrs. T, I'm afraid the letter "I" is not an answer either.

IAN'S MOM: Ahhhhh!

IAN: Wait! Mom—are you crying, or are you saying the letter A?

IAN'S MOM: Ahhhhh!

MERIDEATH: Judges?

IAN: [Scans the room looking for anyone remotely resembling a judge.]

IAN'S MOM: AHHHHH!

MERIDEATH: I've consulted the judges and they concur that your mother, Ian, is indeed suggesting the answer is A, eat off your wrists. But the final answer must be your own.

[Gunfire.]

IAN: MOM!

[A girl's voice wails.]

IAN: SISSY PIE!

[Gunfire.]

IAN: [Drops jaw.]

MERIDEATH: What's it going to be Ian? If you take much longer, I'm afraid we'll have to cut to commercial. And you don't want us to cut anything, do you Ian?

IAN: God, no!

MERIDEATH: Then make a choice.

IAN: A. No C. No…I don't know.

MERIDEATH: Well…there *is* one DeathLine remaining.

IAN: But I wouldn't dare.

MERIDEATH: Are you refusing your DeathLine? Do you know what will happen if you get this question wrong?

IAN: Okay, okay. I'll Mask-the-Audience.

            [Facial gear spills down from the ceiling like party favors, trailing tubing and elastic.]

MERIDEATH: Audience, you know what to do. It's just like in an airplane.

            [Merideath models how to put the mask on. With some prodding by guards here and there, the audience follows suit.]

            Now pick one of the four answers. If you get it wrong, well...

            [A jingle plays as people madly punch buttons.]

MERIDEATH: [A graph pops up.] Overwhelmingly, they pick C, Ian. And those who didn't...

IAN: I know. They get gassed. [Bodies slump to the floor here and there behind him.]

MERIDEATH: Ian finally knows a thing or two! [Laughter.]

IAN: C, huh? Hold your breath forever, eh?

MERIDEATH: 68 percent said C. The audience is usually right. Not always, but usually.

IAN: Is that so?

MERIDEATH: I don't have hard proof. But usually.

IAN: I see...hmm...

MERIDEATH: Are you choosing C?

IAN: I think I'm going to go with C. Hold my breath forever.

MERIDEATH: [Raises an eyebrow.] Is that your final answer?

IAN: [Ian sucks in a lungful of air. Holds it.]

MERIDEATH: [Cocks head.] I asked if that was your final answer.

IAN: [Ian lets it out.] God no!

MERIDEATH: [Merideath's shoulders slump.] Here we go again.

IAN: No we don't.

MERIDEATH: No?

IAN: No! I've finally figured out the right answer! I know how I'm going to get out of this!

MERIDEATH: You do, do you?

IAN: Yes!

MERIDEATH: [Skeptical.] How?

IAN: I'll take the 100 dollars.

MERIDEATH: [Merideath smiles and shakes her head from side to side.]

IAN: [Ian laughs maniacally.]

MERIDEATH: [Merideath makes a throat-slicing gesture. The video cuts to a commercial for Ignorelco Shavers.]

Beyond Undead

The stake plunged into his chest and his life flashed before his eyes: The warm gleam in his mother and father's eyes—reflected in the cold eyes of the vampiress who'd created him. The liquid slide of his first warm kiss—as slick as the bloody underside of flesh between his lips from his last kill. Everything that he loved, he murdered with hatred's hunger. Death became his life: that was the torture of being undead.

His life flashed again before his eyes. So did his death. Over and again. Unending.

This was the torture of his undeath.

Stretch

When I hold my breath the world gets fuzzy and even though my pulse slows down everything around me gets loud, gets fast, gets red, pink, white while my eardrums bow like a trampoline and my cheeks puff out like I'm trying to eat rubber balls and my eyes feel very loose and jiggly inside their sockets—then pop—and I let it go as if my chest were squeezed in the fist of some gargantuan beast but it takes so long to inhale again I can't stand it because the water is too high up too high up and I'm reaching I'm straining I'm praying—I'm breaking the surface—I'm breaking free into the—I'm breaking free—I'm breaking— I'm...floating, face down, arms out-stretched toward some place I'll never reach...eyes peering down at the boat from which I came...lungs full...adrift....

Stress Toy

Hubby opens his birthday gift while Wifey lovingly looks on. He tears open the box. Tilts his head to one side. "What on Earth?"

"It's an executive toy."

"A what?"

"You know—something to keep on your desk. You play with it when you're on the phone or during meetings."

The thing inside the box mewls. Hubby grins and pats the executive toy on the head. "Yes, but what is it, exactly? It's kind of ugly. Not sure I want it on my desk. Won't it make a mess?"

Wifey wraps an arm around Hubby's shoulders. "You'll make everyone jealous, dear! It's a stress reliever—a squeeze toy. It's all the rage on Wall Street this year; it says so right on the box."

"A squeeze toy? You mean I just throttle it and that relieves stress?"

The toy rolls its eyes up at the couple.

They tilt their heads together and smile down at the creature inside.

"Exactly," Wifey says, reaching down into the box and pulling the toy halfway out so the couple can better see its face. "Let me show you."

She squeezes. The executive toy whimpers before its cheeks puff out and its eyes bulge all googly from the squeezing. Its arms and legs swat and swim in the air. Wifey waits until the toy's head turns so purple she can see veins pattern and throb on its scalp.

"See?"

Hubby looks cautiously at Wifey, then back at the suffocating toy. He knew she was stressed-out but her capacity for violence still surprises him. "So you're feeling better now?"

"A little bit," she replies, smiling at him. Then she points with her free hand. "But pay attention to the toy, silly."

The toy's eyes are near popping. Its muscles are tensed and shuddering.

Wifey lets go and drops the toy back into the box.

And then the infant's shoulders sag in relief.

THE DEAD HEAD

I've seen this character time and time again. I try to ignore him, but it's hard. He's making a mockery of me and my partner. Of the uniform. He shouldn't be doing this in public.

The bum with the cruddy brown beard spindles awkwardly in the path behind us, humming some terrible tune. He dances, eyes closed and smiling, caught in his perpetual trance. His psychedelic tie-dye has faded to ruddy brown splotches and soiled gray speckles. His torn jeans are frayed, denim scraping the sidewalk with each sluggish step. His face is haggard; his expression, pained. He stinks like patchouli and pestilence.

My partner gestures with his baton and whispers: "I think *someone's* still living in the 60's."

I swallow my response. That hippie isn't still living in the past. He isn't living at all. I should know. I was the cop who shot him at that anti-war rally.

And still he follows me, spinning away the days till I join him, bearing that creepy smile that rests so peacefully on his face.

My partner starts slapping his stick against his palm. His teeth are gritting. "Let him go, partner," I say, urging him to calm down.

"What are you—some kind of pacifist, like our friend?"

"Some kind," I say, tugging my cap. "Some kind."

The zombie spins behind us. We turn a corner.

The spinner attacks. I passively watch, as I've done a million times.

Returns

The clerk opens his mouth. Then he coughs up a cat. A black one, matted with spit. It claws down his tie and kicks off his chin to land on the counter before springing away with a yelp.

Then the clerk licks his lips the way a working man brushes his hands after a job well done in the dirt.

I am speechless. Instead of asking how the hell he managed to spit out a feline, I try to screw my face into a tighter knot of incredulity. It's his responsibility, I feel, to explain such wacky phenomena.

But in reply to my expression, half of his head puffs up and he eventually spits a pair of garden sheers out of his right ear. I dimly note that they came out handles first; the blades are lacquered with yellow matter.

"Um, I'm just here to return a tie," I say, handing the gift towards him. "But I don't have my receipt."

He farts in reply. Then he lifts up a foot and a chrome jigger falls out from his pants cuff, slimed brown. He raises his other leg and a swizzle stick and whisk spill out. He kicks air and the rest of the bartending set tumbles down his shoe, leaving trails.

My jaw drops.

Someone behind me taps his toes and coughs and harrumphs, impatient for the line to move.

The clerk opens his mouth. It's as large as a pink bread box. He motions at my tie with his tired red eyes.

I feed the gift to him and turn to leave. The guy in the line behind me hands me an acoustic guitar. "You forgot your refund."

I grab it by the soiled neck—strings slippery in my grip—and return to my car, somehow eager to face the holiday traffic.

TASSELS

On all fours, a student bends his head down, baring his neck. On the graduation platform, the learned man in the black robe and hoary white beard raises alma mater's axe high. The announcer calls the student's full name and then the axe blade swings, shearing his head clean off. The flesh is quickly scalped and tasseled before the flayed head is tossed into the tall metal cage that usually holds volleyballs. On the way home from campus, the proud parents dangle the dripping tassel from their rear view mirror, beaming with pride.

Surgical Complications

I'm getting the first dose of meds in pre-op, when the surgeon bursts into my room, stiff-arming a handgun my way. His latex glove crinkles around the handle of his iron instrument. Sweat splotches his paper mask. He's waggling the piece in my face: "I finally know how to save you!"

He cocks the gun and stares down the sights at me. His eyes look crossed; the gray metal becomes his nose, with its one giant nostril flaring over me.

"You're funny," I say, smiling. "And how is shooting me supposed to save me, anyway?"

He twists his head around the barrel at me, puzzling. He eyeballs the morphine drip. "That's right," he says, shoulders calming. "I almost forgot. I'm saving the both of us."

"I don't get it."

He palms his free hand around the muzzle. His eyes clench. He operates.

Jack the Teacher

Mr. Jack's bloodshot eyes were yellow with vein drain, pupils popping, as he shouted at his psychology students. "Okay! All right! I finally admit it! I'm not just Mr. Jack. I'm Mr. Jack the Ripper!" Flamboyantly, he pulled open his blazer and withdrew a crumpled term paper from the inside pocket. Everyone recognized the student's name in the upper corner—a girl who often skipped class. And in red ink, a large letter "F" had been scrawled across the typescript, circled several times. Mr. Jack tore the paper in half. "See? *See?!*"

Stunned, a few students nervously chuckled.

Then the Ripper whimsically tossed the pages in the air, one majestic arm twirl followed by another, before pulling the other side of his coat open like a magician tugging aside a magic curtain. He ceremoniously withdrew a red pen and then dove, puncturing the ribcage of a student in the front row—the one whose paper had been torn to pieces—picking her right up out of her desk with the instrument, screaming "Whore!" when it popped through her back and glimmered ugliness in the fluorescent classroom light. When he dropped her to the floor and hunched down, stepping on her breasts to withdraw his weapon, blood blurted out of her ribcage as though a large boil had been pierced. Then the Ripper began to spin his pen angrily around the wound, circling his grade several times for emphasis.

Stunned, a few students nervously chuckled.

But they were all carrying an "A." Most of the others ran for the door.

He graded the remainder quickly.

LITTLE STOCKING STUFFERS

The kids rush to the fireplace, rubbing the morning crud from their sleepy little eyes. The stockings that hang from the mantle are plump with goodies. Jimmy and Jane can't believe it! They cavort around the mantle, begging father to hand them their gifts. They nearly snatch his hand off when he obeys. The children are so excited, they can barely roll the bloody limb out of its stocking. Little Jimmy gives up trying and sticks his head inside the satin sock like a feedbag. But Jane minds her manners and wipes her chin with a napkin after each and every bite of the lady's foot.

IN THE BALANCE

In the judge's chambers, the man in the long black coat bunches up his sleeve and reaches a bony white arm into a metal cage. He withdraws two rats, dangling by their tails and fighting. On a nearby scale, he places one on each side of the balance. One side is labeled "innocent"; the other "guilty." The judge releases them, and waits, eager to decide the life sentence.

₪IAGARA

You may have noted the deplorable state of our cultural environ-
ment lately. You could blame the other political party, but there is a
scientific explanation for what you are seeing.

They live among us. They pose inside our bodies and use our
flesh as their masks. Worse than the pod people in the movies, these
masters of disguise have overtaken our easily tricked and gullible
autonomic system—the part of our body that works on commands
preprogrammed into our brains—the part that dilates our eyes and
keeps our diaphragm moving and heart beating. But they do not
interfere with those bodily needs—oh, no—they require them to mask
their assault. They are small and need to multiply in order to win their
battle against us. They are smart little buggers. They don't take over
the whole body; they just parasitically infest us until the time is right
for their coming. And they know how to hide in plain sight: they live
in one and only one area where they can engage in secret commune:
the sex organs. That's right—the reproductive system. And they
reward us for obeying their needs to communicate and replicate by
sending pleasure signals to the brain. That's how they spread and
become legion. And if you don't obey their demands, they punish you
with anxiety and frustration that leads to stress which leads to…you
know what.

So now do you understand? It is a national emergency and I am
on a mission to stop them. Will you join me? They live among us. They
hide inside you and me. I can no longer allow them to control me, or
control you. The stakes are too high. And as I have learned in my
research the only way to stop them—aside from suicide—is to
imprison them for good. Cut off their contact from each other.

Abstinence, Mr. President, is very difficult to enforce but we must
enforce it through extreme measures. The public will resist but it takes
a leader like you to make such difficult decisions. I have attached a

very thorough document outlining one possible way to combat sexual commerce among the masses. It describes a medicinal compound I have invented which not only decreases the sex drive but also mutates the reproductive organs in a way that eventually seals off all tubes, holes and ducts. I have codenamed this compound "Diagara"—hah-hah!—but I send you my research (see attached) in all seriousness. In the event that this is not a cost effective solution, direct measures may be required. I leave such mass enforcement planning in your hands. I trust you to do what's best for the citizens of our fine country. As for me, I have already done my part.

Dutifully yours, Doe Johnson, M.D., Ph.D.

Strange Trout

The freshwater fish flops on my fine china plate in a puddle of scaly gray water too hot to be pond scum. Slit at the belly and pried open in a fine fillet, the trout still somehow manages to turn his silver eyeball up at me.

He thwats his bony white tail at my fork whenever I pierce his innards, spilling his steaming guts out all on his own. He is his own anchovy can key.

Meanwhile my cat impatiently waits at my feet, gently batting his own tail, curious about the strange new toy from which I feed him morsels to quench the anticipation clearly evident all over his drooling white skull.

Revenge of the Mummy

A mangled body drains life into Egyptian sand. The pharaoh peels and offers the thief his brittle gauze. Laughter fills the tomb.

NIGHTMARE JOB #2

I'm the taster for the king. Every sip could be poison. Every bite could be ground glass.

The king plays it safe as any king should, 'tis true, but my liege is also quite insane. He makes me taste things that no one in their right mind would ever put in his mouth: dead insects found belly-up on windowsills; soiled fabrics; the liquids sloshing in piss pots and spittoons.

But I obey my master. I would die to save him.

He's not only crazy—he's often suicidal. "Taste this first," he says, handing me a flask full of green smoke. I pretend to slurp the witch's potion and clutch my throat and feign death, dropping the bottle to the ground, shattering it so he won't even have the chance to kill himself with the vile poison.

I come back from the dead the following day, but he doesn't realize it. He is still insane. What happens one moment is forgotten in the next. And he never adds it up that he could simply forgo the usage of a taster and off himself with ease. Even his own illogicality is lost on him.

But one day he slips. When I arrive in his chamber, he is already eating a ham hock without my first tasting of it. It has a green tinge around the bone. The king's eyes are dilated enough to fill the hairy aperture of lid that surrounds them. Sluggishly, he passes a large ham hock my way and says "You mush tashte dis virsht."

I obey my master. I would die to save him.

I snap my jaws down on his wrist and swallow the poisonous blood that pollutes his mind. He drops the hock. Then *he* drops.

I stare at the limb on the stone floor before me, and try not to swallow.

IN THE MIDDLE

The hallway is empty, save for one teenager who approaches me. He is large, trucker-size, sweating. He wears a black T-shirt emblazoned with three words:

Sex. Murder. Art.

The words are stacked with sex on top and art on the bottom. Murder's in the middle.

He passes me by. I know he just left art class. I heard that today they would be exposed to their first nude model. But it's only 11:17— class shouldn't be over yet. Perhaps he finished early. His footsteps echo down the empty hall like the period after each word. I follow him.

The Seven-Headed Beast

The beast has seven heads and seven sets of teeth. The first head has no eyes, but sees through its nose. It can conjure a semblance of shape through scent, so it knows just where to bite. The second head has twenty necks—a mesh of fleshy tubes cabling up to the brain. All lead back to its heart. Some think this makes it easier to kill, but they die mistaken, for each neck can dodge the blade like a cobra. The third head is small red swab of gummy flesh, no bigger than a pink marshmallow. It absorbs whatever it touches and chews with a manic urgency from somewhere deep inside its pillow of raw tissue. The fourth head is long dead and flaccid on the stalk of its purple neck, but its eyes still live and stare and will drive a man mad if he makes contact. The fifth head is a death dry skeleton's skull that's puppeteered by a jaundiced wet hand that reaches through its vacant neckhole and throws a demonic voice. The sixth head is a beautiful medusa, whose flesh is a patchwork of scales, whose phallic skeletal asps slither into her sockets and out from her lilac lips and sometimes they have to fight their way out of the knots they create on her scalp, shedding their skin in the struggle. The seventh head is mine, which contains—and releases—them all. My head hinges and falls backward at the jawline and all of them wrestle for attention. They think they control me, but forget that I could champ down at just the right time and kill us all.

Psycho Hunter

He's a madman in plaid flannel. They say he roams the forest, bearded like sasquatch, still wearing his reflective safety vest and camouflaged cap. They say you can recognize him from the blood splatter on the plastic.

He moves from kill to kill, feeding off the men he slays and stealing their ammo for the next time. The cops hunt the hunter, but all they find are body parts strewn in his wake—sometimes limbs smoldering in campfires, other times heads with gnawed necks lopsided on the ground with hollowed out holes where he sucked the eyes and tongue meat out. During their nightly camps, the posse trades rumors about what might have triggered the psycho hunter's madness. One sheriff speculates that the crazy man plumb forgot to bring his brain medication with him to the woods—that simple. Another ponders whether he might be possessed by Indian spirits. Another thinks he's the bastard son of the Son of Sam.

But I know the truth: a bullet grazed his skull and that was all it took to set him off.

And that as he tears through the flesh of all these woodland campers, the only thing he's hunting for is me. For revenge.

They say it's not good sport to shoot a wounded animal, unless you're putting it out of its misery.

I can't wait until we find him.

A WORSE MOUSETRAP

As I type, the mouse climbs my shoulder and leaps into my breast pocket. I laugh when his furry gray head pops out. He twitters his whiskers, watching as I finish my apology. I hug him against my heart. Later, I will sign my note while the rat poison makes its way through my system.

Little Devils

My neighbor runs a daycare, and she must be good at it because I rarely hear the little yappers. Except during playtime, that is—an hour of free play in the backyard while the woman cooks lunch. The children run out the back door like it was recess at school and chew up every inch of her yard, which is thankfully well-fenced in. They play the usual childhood games and sometimes, as a distraction, I like to watch. But I usually regret it.

The woman has a mannequin set up in the backyard—apparently from her old job at the mall—which they like to torture and dismember. The kids pull the doll's arms off and use them as ball bats, pitching the head and smacking it across the yard. They take the rest of the body off its stand and dance with the decapitated body, its legs flailing like they were alive and kicking in pain. Sometimes they tear off the legs and have swordfights with them, no matter how floppy at the knees. The torso is a sled they drag around behind them, taking turns on the ribcage ride. Other times it's a kicking bag they seek to flatten with their little feet.

Every night my neighbor puts the mannequin back together. She calls him Daddy.

LATEX

A rubber glove lies on the rest room tile, two fingers flattened like they're counting. You first assumed the janitor was forgetful. Now you imagine a more sinister purpose. You dare to touch it. You slide the latex over your hand, and it fits as snugly as someone else's flesh.

MOTHER'S HAUNTED HOUSECOAT

Skeletal fingers pop the housecoat buttons—plunking open the sick red nipplets on the robe—which squish wetly the way an eardrum bursts in your head. Rotting in this closet for aeons, this new mother pulls me toward her gaping wound of a chest. I wail infantile in the abyss of the dark space inside and my voice echoes for as long as I've been alive. In the blank depth of her body I see my child-self— the cells I left behind, long festering inside her. In a flash it squirms in the miasmic womb of tar and gathers the sound of my voice into its suckling purple lips. It swallows my echo into its belly-sac—a pustule that bloats into the size of a fist and I marvel at the life-giving power of my voice. But this means I cannot stop screaming. Until suddenly I feel my lungs tugging out through my windpipe and scraping out through my mouth. The choice is simple in this tug of war: either bite or give my life over to the self I could have been.

And then I realize that I already have.

Mother buttons her housecoat up and the wound seals out the light in a mucousy haze. I close my eyes, likewise, and prepare to fester in my winter hibernation.

INSIDE THE MAN
WITH NO EYELIDS

Blindness is not merely an absence of sight. For me it is a preponderance of vision—too much at once, clogging the rods and cones, an overdose of light and geometric contours, the reflection of two mirrors face-to-face infinite like the damp and drying surface of my eyes rubbing against the sandpaper friction of the world before me.

The only lubricant is tears. You do not realize that you are always crying, always lamenting life because it is covered by your fleshy lids which bat and wipe and flicker the glaze we see through. The glaze that is my window. My doorway to the soul never cleansed. Forever open. Drying out like a mat after a nocturnal Indian summer storm, steaming in the unseen morning.

I do not cry in pain. I have seen it all—I can ignore nothing. Jaded by visions of other people's eyes winking, I do not turn away, but other people's pupils evade my own. They wince at the scabs that encircle my vision like insane and horrid living lips on the eyepiece of binoculars which could suck out your brains. They see my eyes dilating over their own reflection within the strained veins that web my vitreous as if entrapped there, which they are: forever branded, I am unable to purge away any image.

I can no longer differentiate between sleep and wake—my eyes never close, never shut out the world, never tighten the escape hatch for dreams to curdle in the brain. Visions fade in and out like cut-frame montage and I am trapped forever within the theatre; I do not know what is real and what is imagined. I do not know if I am awake or asleep. And therefore, I know nothing. Except sight, seeing.

And dust. Motes gather like snowflakes sponging into puddles and congeal to skin on the surface of my vision. A manic storm outside.

I exit this house and cock my head skyward, neck impossible, horizontal. I allow rain to pool in my double empty lakes, overflowing. Each drop is a bullet to the brain: *cap-ish-cap-ish-cap-ish*. Thunder rumbles in my ears—too distant—and I wish for lightning to strike, to animate the dust still clouding sight: whether to both blind or birth hairy flaps of flesh. So I can no longer see.

So I can no longer dream you, there, listening with gutted ear canals, touching me with your skinless bones and slick muscles and pulsing organs, speaking, screaming without tongue or throat right now. This moment. Inside me. Alive.

Burning Bridges

Because I am a surgeon, it is difficult for me to kill you.

No, it's not a moral difficulty. I am sworn to the Hippocratic Oath—to save life whenever I'm able. And by killing you, I'll save millions.

My problem is that there are so *many* tools at my disposal that I am overwhelmed by all the possible choices!

Shiny trays full of saws and scalpels, scissors and syringes...this operating room is like a toy chest. How can I properly make you suffer, like my poor Karen? A million instruments at my disposal, yet nothing will quite do.

I've picked shotgun shrapnel out of a man's brain and thought of your open skull beneath my forceps. I've sutured sucking chest wounds and imagined that it was your last hot breaths pouring across the back of my fingers. I've shocked flatline patients with paddles and dreamed I was pressing them fully amped against your eyelids. But none of these ideas seem quite...just.

Even when I injected that syringe into your neck and brought you here, I wasn't quite sure what I would do. Your cigarettes killed my daughter—not even twenty-one years old. You bastard. I'd blow up your whole damned corporate office if I had it in me. But I know *you* are entirely to blame. You're the bottom line man. The guy who makes a living off the dying.

You deserve cancer, like Karen, but I don't have time to wait for it. Too kind, anyway. I thought maybe I'd asphyxiate you—shove a tailpipe into your bony little mouth and start the car. Or maybe just strangle you with these latex-gloved hands. But after I tossed those all-too-common ideas aside, I knew one thing: *you must choke.* Just like my little Karen did. Once I settled on that, the rest sort of came to me.

Wait.

Here. Put this cigarette inside your mouth. Think of it as a last wish. Just like the firing squad. I'll even undo your belts. You can't escape anyway. Go ahead. Smoke.

You see, I didn't only snip your vocal cords while you were out. I perforated the major nerve cluster that controls your diaphragm. Not all the way through—just little Morse Code cuts, really, along with a little rigging with dissolving suture. Your diaphragm is hanging on by a few thin threads right now. Every breath you take frays the binding a little more, like a rope bridge threatening to snap beneath each footstep. There's nothing you can do to stop or control it. Can't breathe softly or slowly or shallow…nothing. Time will kill you.

I know you believe deep down in your gut that you didn't kill Karen. She made a choice, right? She knew the risks.

Well, then.

I didn't kill you, either. It's your body that's turned against you, not me.

Scalpels are over there. I'll let you make your own choices.

I'll lock the door behind me. Enjoy your smoke.

TAKING CARE OF BABY

The baby monitor blares.

He steamrolls over to my side of the bed, tapping: "Babe, will you *please* shut that thing up?"

I shuffle into the nursery to feed and cuddle my boy. He's a noisy one. He keeps me up but I don't mind. I hope to hear his first words.

* * *

The baby monitor blares.

He screams from the box beneath my garden bed, pounding: "Babe, will you *please* open this thing up?"

I roll over and cuddle his pillow. He's a noisy one. He'll keep me up but I don't mind. I hope to hear his last words.

Five Mean Machines

Dreamachinery

Suffering from a bout of recurring nightmares, my wife bought a machine that harvests dreams. Every night she goes through a purging routine. After a brief moment of wrestling with the metal cobra she has brought to our bed, she slips it over her temple and turns it on. The thing vibrates and thrums, making surprisingly loud noises, sounding something like an elevator chamber while I toss and turn beside her, waiting for her to get off.

Though I couldn't find the box it came in, she says it's called "Dreamachinery." She says it helps her sleep better and though I want her to get rid of the obnoxiously loud thing, I jealously capitulate, understanding why she would want to escape the land of nightmares. But I wonder where all those dreams have really gone. I ask her this and she smugly says, "John, dear, you think too much." I ask if I can borrow the device, thinking that maybe it will help me think less. She kisses me to change the subject as though I'd told a really bad joke.

One night I do manage to sleep soundly but in the morning I find she's disappeared. The Dreamachinery is coiled beside me like an alien stethoscope, heavy and sunken into the down of her pillow. I pull the device over my head and can still feel her warmth on the prods that penetrate my ears. Clutching a metal cylinder against my chest, I hold on to it like a Walkman, but can find no play button or rewind dials. I wonder if I'll find her inside there somewhere. If she'll even want to come back from wherever it is I'm going. If she'll let me in. I wonder if I'll even be able to return.

Fear now keeps me awake. Recalling my wife's nightly routine, I figure that I have to fall asleep and conjure dreams to make the damned harvester work. But how can I pull the cord to start my own dream engine without her? How can I sleep with a hangman's noose around my neck, waiting for the floor to drop out? I give up hope. On my capacity to dream. On my desire to be my wife's savior. I give up hope on hope and maybe she, too, felt this way as she disappeared.

I move my arms to take off the Dreamachinery and try to slip it out of my ear canals. But its metallic prongs pinch my forehead in protest and I now know that I have been wearing this dream harvester all along. It whirrs gelid in my ears and licks into my lobes telling me so. I loosen my grip on its snaking cables. I let the blades swing. I let the scythes fall. I'm gone.

Womachine

She pistons inside me with plunger parts no one can see, churning my blood in her secret circulation of wire and electroplated metal piping. Her engine sparks below my hood. She shudders in my chassis. A screw flies loose and I run right into another one on the road, meshing into her grille, shattering her glass and turning twisting tumbling into a hunk of monstrous junk, my body worthless, rent unrecognizable. But somewhere in the wreck she still purrs.

Trimachine

The barber told me that for an extra hundred dollars, I could get free haircuts for life. As he buzzed the edge of the back of my neck, I looked at myself in the mirror and tried to do the math. I quickly saw how good a bargain it would be, so long as the barber didn't close shop and leave town.

"It's a deal," I said and he smugly smiled, clicking off the electric clippers and reaching for the long handlebars of a strange machine nearby that I hadn't paid any attention to. It was like a floor buffer, turned upside-down—heavy and cumbersome in his grip. He moved it toward me.

"What's that?"

"My invention. It cuts your hair once and makes it stay the same length for life." He moved the contraption toward my head.

I pulled back. "Wait! How's it work?"

He cocked his head to one side. "I can't answer that. That would be giving away my stock in trade."

I looked at the machine again. I didn't see any blades or trimmers. "Have you tested this before?"

"Of course! On myself!"

I looked at his hairline. He was right—I'd never seen it any other way. Of course, I assumed this was because he was keeping it well-groomed, as all barbers do. But perhaps his weird barbering machine accounted for his perfect hairline.

"Okay," I said, leaning back in the chair and sizing up my bangs. "Maybe an inch off the top. That would be great."

"I need you to be perfectly still," he said, and asked me to put on a chin strap that suddenly came around my face from somewhere behind the barber chair.

"Um…okay." I slipped it on.

"Ready?"

"Yeth," I said, the chinstrap keeping my jaw tight. "Let 'er rip."

The machine seized my scalp and began to twist.

The barber adjusted his flesh toupee and smiled.

Stomachine

The worker willingly stuck his hand into the machine.

A long rectangular blade slammed down with unforgiving certainty, taking it clean off at the wrist.

Blood spit out across the large panel of glass that allowed workers to examine the inner workings of the machine. The exposed wheels and cogs lewdly ground behind the bloody splatter above them. Behind the glass, row after row of product fed through the automatic conveyance, oblivious to the human tragedy nearby. The machine's unseen engine whined as it worked on the man's dismembered limb with metal pincers, the white fingers virtually signing for help as the mechanism rent the digits at the knuckles and folded the palm into an impossible origami of flesh.

The worker slumped to the floor, gripping the throb of his stump, somehow amazed by his own mechanics. The exposed bone pizza where his hand should have been was a puddle of ice, steaming with life vapors in the chilly room. His opened arteries shot more blood with every quick race of his pulse, but the pressure he put on his slippery wrist managed to slow his progress toward death. Part of him wanted to bite down on the meatus, to chew the circles of vein closed like straws between his teeth, but there were too many of them.

And he knew better. He was just in shock. He had to be. He caught his reflection—pale as a hospital trashcan liner—ghosting the glass windowpane on the machine. He felt hungry. Empty.

Soon the machine's engine stopped whining and grinding. Something grumbled like a stomach. Two coins plunked into a bucket. Green digits blinked a phrase: "Sold Out."

The worker reached into the coin return with his phantom hand before falling to the floor. The thin metal flap there snapped back and bit the air where his index finger would have been. He laughed as he bled and released his wrist. The fresh blood warmed the wound.

A newly wrapped product dropped into its proper place behind the line of others, ready to eat.

Mortichinery

A man had to bury a wife. But he did not want to.

So when the mortician was making preparations for the open casket viewing, and the man saw how beautiful his lost wife had become when embalmed—her cheeks more rosy than when she was young, her eyes transfixed with mascara she'd never worn before, her hair permed in unfamiliar curls—he asked whether there were some way to keep her so perfect.

"Your compliments are too kind, sir. My humble goal is that she will always remain this way," the well-dressed mortician said as he straightened his tie. "In your memories."

"But that's not good enough," the man mumbled, still lovingly gazing down upon the mannequin his wife had become. "Memories fade like old Polaroids." He gently fingered his wife's stiff, dead hand. "And so does flesh. But I want my wife to be with me—like this—forever."

The mortician could tell that the macabre man was earnest and took pity on him. He decided to at last reveal his secret experiment. "The problem is not the processes of death," he said, leading the man to a private and hidden chamber beneath the mortuary. "It's the low quality of embalming fluid. It needs to be constantly renewed and replenished to keep the dead alive, as it were. So I have invented a device which keeps pumping the carcass with enough fluid to maintain a healthy body." They rounded a turn at the foot of the stairs and inspected a large wooden sarcophagus enmeshed in a network of brass tubes and red wires and metallic buckets.

Noticing his puzzlement, the mortician said: "It's a chamber that perpetually embalms the subject. It uses the circulatory system already in place to keep the tissues replenished by pumping fluid through the veins and arteries at a steady rate of speed. It works, almost, like an external heart—and, indeed, I have borrowed some of the mechanical parts from transfusion equipment. I first called it 'The Circulatory Coffin' but that was too scientific-sounding. So now I just call it 'The Mortichine.'" The mortician's face flushed with blood as he toyed with a nearby spigot. "I'm not sure if that name is sexy enough to sell to the mainstream market, and it's obviously still in development, but..."

The man saw the genius behind the device immediately, despite its messy tangle of unkempt tubes. He slapped the mortician on his bony back: "Well, I call it 'brilliant!'" He paced around the casket, examining the metal prods that lined the floor of the box like a postmodern bed of nails. "I assume it works? That you've tested it on others?"

"Yes," the mortician said, still wincing from the back slap and nodding solemnly. "On my own daughter."

"I'm sorry," the man said.

They stared down at the contraption in silence, understanding one another perfectly.

"Amber killed herself. Slashed her wrists. Luckily, I'm as good a thread man as I am a fluid man."

The man nodded.

Time passed.

"So when can you do it?" the man finally asked, looking up at his new friend. "And how much will it cost me?"

The process was quite expensive, because the constant replenishment of fluids would be a pricey affair. But the man realized he was rich enough in insurance to afford it. Arrangements were quickly made to substitute another corpse for the wife's burial and they decided to keep the embalmed woman in the mortician's hidden room. It was impossible, they agreed, to keep the wife in the man's own home because of maintenance requirements, not to mention the suspicion it might cause. It would take two weeks to prepare The Mortichine and make it suitable for regular viewing—after that waiting period, the man would be welcome to come and go as he pleased.

The day finally arrived for his first visit. The man and the mortician chatted like old friends as they entered the hidden chamber, then went into a back room where there were several stainless steel doors with large padlocks bolted onto them. The mortician pulled a ring of keys from his pocket and opened one of the locks, unveiling a finely wall-papered room with a flower arrangement and two leather chairs arranged around a fine mahogany coffin. The casket was closed. All was quiet, save for the sound of the pulsing machinery that regularly pumped and sloshed like a rubbery heartbeat. "Do you approve?"

"Approve?" He clapped the mortician on the back again. "My good man, this is beyond my expectations!"

"Then allow me to unveil your beloved wife." The mortician pulled open the casket lid like a bellhop would open the doorway to a penthouse suite.

The man's wife glowed with a pallor of fluids and fresh make-up. She wore the fine cocktail dress the man had provided (one of many that would be routinely changed each week) and her eyes were open and gleaming. She looked even more life-like than she had two weeks ago. The Mortichine had done—was still doing—a fine job.

The husband nearly fell to the ground, but then caught himself on the coffin base. He stood and looked down upon his wife. "Her eyes. They are so...so..."

"Real?"

"No...different."

"Yes, they are. Her eyes are made of glass, I'm afraid, so the color isn't a perfect match. As a matter of fact, I couldn't keep all her organs replenished with proper fluids. Her brain, too, is all cotton, I'm sorry to say. As is her lung cavity. Other amenities and tailor fitting had to be performed elsewhere, suffice it to say that I went through a lot of thread. But the circulatory system is rather intact, I assure you." The mortician looked at the man and then realized he really didn't want to hear any of these details. For the mortician, the science was the beauty, not the finished product. But he tried to make it up to the man anyway: "Look at her flesh, or better yet, her lips...see how full they are? See how perfect?"

The man did. He bent at the waist and then kissed the cold meat of her face. Her cheek was so firm with fluid that he could feel it pulsing against his lips.

The mortician clasped his hands, cocked his head, and sighed with satisfaction.

When he looked over at the man for confirmation, however, he saw the unimaginable. He towered over the casket with his arms upraised, a large carving knife glinting in his two-fisted grip. Before the mortician could cry "No!" the man was in motion, plunging the blade hard into his wife's ribcage. Black ooze blurted out from an aortic tear and splattered up his sleeve before he repeated the atrocity, stabbing deep into the chest again. Liquids began pissing out all over the box.

Though he knew he would do better to run, the mortician dropped helplessly to his knees: "My work!"

Again the man stabbed into the coffin, this time plunging his blade down into his wife's throat. The voice box gargled as if there were some life inside the larynx. With two fists the man twisted it around to silence her.

The mortician could no longer stand the grotesque sounds blurting and scraping above him. He pulled himself to the man's side and began tugging on his pant leg. "Please! Stop! I implore you!"

The man stopped and breathed heavily above him. The Mortichine began making sucking sounds from somewhere in the room. A hose popped somewhere but the machinery kept chugging along.

The man turned to look down at the mortician. He smiled and patted his head. "It's all right." He stabbed the knife into the body once more and then left it pegged there, standing like a stake in wet soil. "I don't think I hit the actual device."

"Why are you doing this?" the mortician cried from the floor, calming a bit. "I thought we had an understanding!"

"We still do, my good man," the husband said, looking back into his wife's unblinking eyes with some satisfaction, noting dark droplets resting on the glass. "We still do. You use that magic sewing talent of yours to patch up my wife and keep her ripe and juicy for me." He flicked at the blade handle in her belly like it was a tuning fork, making it wobble. "And I'll be back every week to kill this fucking bitch all over again."

The mortician could feel his eyes trembling in their sockets as tears spilled over the rims.

"And if you don't do it, I'll come back and cut you, instead." He pulled the knife from his wife's body with a tug and then squatted down to confront him face-to-face. "And then there wouldn't be anyone left around here to put Humpty Dumpty back together again. Understand?"

The mortician bowed his head away and stared at the floor, where brown-gold embalming fluid pooled around his feet. It didn't look like blood but it certainly spilled like it. "Yes," he said, seeing destiny. "I do."

The man patted the mortician on his head like a good boy and then stood up. "That's what my wife said once, too." He chuckled and then gripped his blade tightly, stabbing the air as if reliving the atrocity he'd committed, still wanting more. "Now why don't you show me where you keep that daughter of yours?"

He was stunned by the audacity of this request—the realization that the man would not be satisfied with just one body was more chilling than what he had just witnessed—but the mortician knew better than to resist. Mechanically, he pulled himself up, still staring at the puddle of amber liquid on the floor. Then, despondently, he marched the man back to the hallway and led him toward his daughter's chamber. The stainless steel door was padlocked and the mortician nervously jangled the key ring, trying to find the right match.

"C'mon, hurry up," the man said, wiping his blade on his pant leg.

The mortician shook, dropping the keys.

"Idiot! Don't bother!" The man bent forward and picked them up and impatiently moved to open the door himself. After three tries, he found the key that fit and quickly unhasped the lock. He kicked open the door. The room was dark, dank. He couldn't see the coffin at all as he entered, but instead encountered glints of familiar looking equipment.

"It stinks in here. Where's the freaking light?" the man asked, but the mortician was already rushing toward him, knocking him forward into the dark, tripping him headfirst over the edge of the coffin. The man tumbled forward, slashing madly at air, knocking over an intravenous bottle instead before slamming face-first into a large thick needle in the middle of the casket. This needle was intended to tap into the aorta of the deceased, but it popped into the man's throat with a wheeze. The remainder of his body fell into the battery of smaller needles that lined the bed of the contraption like a modern day Iron Maiden.

As life began pouring out of him from hundreds of holes, he felt the press of old meat and rust into his guts. The room's fluorescent lights flickered on. The mortician pressed a button and the needles shunted more deeply into him, tickling his inner organs so far inside that he quivered and gasped with something terribly similar to laughter.

"I do so very much appreciate your support of my research, sir." He turned a dial and thick liquid began pumping into the man's flaccid neck, coursing down his throat. "You might appreciate this new device, as well. You see, it not only keeps the flesh lively…" he placed a finger over a large green button, "but it also takes care of all the stitching and body tailoring I would normally have to do myself. It's kind of like a sewing machine, I suppose. It should save me a lot of work." He looked over at the dying man in his coffin. "But I'm not certain. I haven't tested it yet. I certainly wouldn't try it out on my daughter, I assure you."

He pressed the green button and all the needles began to writhe and stitch and staple the man's organs together. "I wonder what to call this one…the Rigor Rigger? The Deader Threader? Hmm…"

A bone scraped, sounding like a file sliding on porcelain. The pelvis cracked in half with a meaty snap. The liver popped and was smeared against the abdominal wall by a metal fork, staining the body from the inside out. Liquid overflowed in a nearby drainage bucket.

The mortician didn't hear these things, even though he had left the door ajar. He was too busy brainstorming as he visited his daughter in her finely decorated chamber, one door over.

Tugging the Heartstrings

When Dad came home from the hospital, he had little black knots and strings of suture left in his chest. They ran up his ribcage as if his flesh were a bodice that had been tightly bound to the bone. They were straining to hold him together.

I found out about this when I jumped into his arms upon his return from the hospital. As I dove up to him, he winced and almost fell before softening and holding me tight. Dad did everything tough, even going soft. I went limp and he clutched me like a flimsy pillow. Then I felt the lumps against my chest like hard buttons on a coat. Over his shoulder, I saw my mother's eyes scolding me.

He held me tight. He could die but he loved me more than that. He didn't let go until we both noticed the wetness seeping into my shirt. I pried myself away like a bandage. We both pretended not to notice the bloodstains or the hospital smells. But mother panicked, ushering him to the recovery bed she'd set up in their bedroom and reprimanded me with a familiar scrunched up look.

Mom put him in a bathrobe that became his uniform for the next two months of his recovery. During that time, he brought us all closer together. His heart surgery had the same effect on our family that my bicycle accident had at age six. I'd fallen into a ravine on my way home from school and broke my leg in two places. I would have died if a passer-by hadn't spotted me down there, writhing in pain. Mom and Dad fawned over me for weeks after that, as if spending more time with me after the accident would make up for not preventing it.

In spite of the pain, those were good times for me. Mom took me to see a lot of movies, despite my chunky cast and the awkwardness of crutches. Dad spent an entire Saturday making a montage of images on my cast: butterflies fluttering around planets and stars inside of caves that opened up to mountain vistas towering over fields littered with flowers...and on and on. A hall-of-mirrors effect everywhere. It was the first time I'd really seen him draw and it was so good that I let him cover up the dumb graffiti my school friends had made. And I remember dying to see what he had drawn on the underside of my thigh, a place just out of my sight.

Later, I'd discovered he'd drawn butterflies and portraits of him and me.

I wanted to show him that I loved him just as much now. I read stories to him at night. He'd smile as he nodded off in his leather recliner.

But whenever I saw his exposed chest I was reminded that the damage was permanent. A tattoo of shiny pink tissue was branded on his torso in the shape of a huge capital letter "H." It would show whenever the lapels of his flannel bathrobe loosened like some sort of superhero costume he'd been secretly wearing all along. He'd pour his coffee and the bathrobe would part and I'd hear a cartoon voice in my head saying, "The coffeepot is nearly empty! This looks like a job for Healingman!"

One night, though, I closely examined the scar as he slept in his recliner. He wasn't healing the way I'd assumed. There was still one knot of suture at the top right arm of that big H. It was disgustingly black beneath his hairy left nipple. Insectoid. Dad had gone in once to have them removed but somehow—bafflingly—they missed one.

One morning he walked into the kitchen in his bathrobe and the black knot peeked out at me with the audacity of a bloated tick. I wanted to pull it like a zipper. I summoned the courage to bring it up. "They missed a stitch, Dad."

He eyed me over his coffee cup. "Don't want to go back to the hospital."

"That's nuts," I said, eating a banana to slow down my mouth. "I know it hurts to get them removed, but you don't want to risk getting infected."

He pulled his flannel tight over his chest. Raised his stubbly chin. "I told the doctor to leave it in."

Slimy banana spilled out of my mouth like baby food: "What?"

He nodded as if affirming a commitment. "I wanted to remember what happened."

"You've gotta be kidding me. What doctor would do such a thing?" I made a father-son-and-holy-ghost gesture at his scar. "And isn't all of that enough of a walk down memory lane?"

He held up his hand. "No, not the surgery." His eyes turned warm and milky: like hot chocolate. "Afterward."

I didn't understand what any of it meant until the day I looked down at his casket two weeks later and saw that suture knot. It was black and hard as a nail's head beneath the white tuxedo shirt Mom had put on him. He wanted to remember the hug I'd given him. The one where I loved him so hard he bled and it didn't matter.

I reached down and teased the knot like a nipple before I pinched it beneath the fabric and pulled the suture free.

A stain of fluid oozed into a pattern that quickly found the ravines of his scar and eventually unfurled its color across his chest—a butterfly spreading its red wings wide.

Face of Clay

A child plunges pink clay through a sausage grinder of plastic. She pie-pans the dough, molding a face. She dubs the cookie of clay "Mark"—same name as her older brother. It bears a likeness: the tee-peed eyebrows, the horsey nostrils, the drippy frown. Mark's face, frozen in that expression he'd get when he was mad at Mommy and taking it out on his sister.

"Just playing," he'd say and let go when tears spilled from her bruised eyes.

Now there is only this silent clay. This fleshy mash she pokes and pummels and plays with before grinding it again.

Blind Spot

The homeless man's Seeing Eye Dog is also his Smelling Nose, leading him to tonight's freshest dinner. Unfortunately, it's not his tasting mouth.

CRUSTY OLD AGE

Before dawn, an old woman forks holes into a flaky piecrust, cooling down the steaming tin on her windowsill.

Outside, a lurking vampire responds. In a burst of blackened dust, he transforms into a cloud of fruit flies and drifts into her opened window. Absent-mindedly, she swats as he reassumes shape.

She tastes of lilac as he bites a frail freckled shoulder, but her runny tissue is warm over his tongue like baked fruit. She too will develop a taste for human pie, baked by time. Brittle bones and dentures won't prevent her; she knows how to use a fork.

NEXT-DOOR

Arnold turned from the shining metal box, presenting his new ware to Fred like Vanna White. "So what do you think?"

Fred raised an eyebrow. "It doesn't look all *that* different from most microwave ovens." Arnold's cat, a beat up tabby, began rubbing his leg and he kicked it away.

"Oh, but it is." Arnold smiled. "It's state of the art. You can't buy something like this at your local department store, ya know."

Fred took a swig from a beer. "Sure, Arnie. It doesn't even have any of those fancy buttons..."

"It's remote controlled. Believe me, Fred. This is the best microwave oven in the country. It has as much wattage and power as, hell, I dunno...the space shuttle!"

Fred rolled his eyes. "You must have one hell of an electric bill then."

"Oh, I don't use it that often. But when I do, it's well worth it. Did you know that this thing can fry an *entire* chicken in less than thirty seconds? Yup. And it'll come out as juicy as if ya cooked it in an oven all day. Even better."

Fred finished off his beer and stared speechless at his neighbor.

"You can even put aluminum in it! Tin cans, plates, glasses...anything. All it cooks is the food. It's amazing!"

"Uh-huh."

"Don't believe me?"

"Sure, I do." Fred was sick of Arnold's tireless self-absorption. Every time Arnold got something new, he invited Fred over to gloat. If it wasn't his fuel injection lawnmower, it was his new and improved electric barbecue. Always, Arnold would say "top of the line," which really translated into "a helluva lot better than anything you've got, Fred."

But Fred always had one up on Arnold, as well. Arnold's wife.

And *she* was top of the line. He'd had numerous affairs with her and after she got a taste of ol' Freddy boy, she left Arnold and his cat for good, in search of a life without the domestic bullshit. As far as Fred knew, Arnold had no clue why she left him, and that suited him just fine. He missed her, but he could always take consolation in the truth whenever Arnold tried to prove how much better he was than his neighborhood pal.

Fred smirked. "Still doesn't beat home cookin'."

"I couldn't agree more," Arnold said, his throat erupting in horrendous laughter.

"What the hell are you laughing at? If you like home cooking so damned much, why'd you buy the stupid thing?"

"Listen, wanna try it out?" Arnold asked, ignoring Fred's comment.

"No, Arnie, I don't have very much time..."

Arnold took a remote control out from his pocket and pressed a button, causing the door on the microwave to click open. Then he chuckled, bending over to pick up Whiskers, his cat, from the ceramic tiled floor. He placed the cat inside the metallic box and slammed the door.

"What? You've gotta be crazy!" Fred stared at Arnold in disbelief.

Arnold giggled, savoring every second. "With this fancy remote, I can turn it on from way over here," he said, walking out of the kitchen and into an adjacent living room.

"Not if I can help it." Fred walked over to the microwave oven and searched for a button to open the door. Not finding one, he began nervously prying at the door's edges. "Damn it, Arnie, this isn't funny!"

Arnie's voice was distant: "I can even turn it on from outside, Fred."

"Arnie! You love this cat! What are you doing!"

Sweat beaded on Fred's brow. He madly punched at the oven, denting its shiny chrome frame. The cat inside meowed and Fred's heart missed a beat. With wild eyes he looked for the cord to pull the plug and...

Fred's eyes popped out of their sockets as his innards instantaneously boiled. His skin dried, bubbled, cracked; the muscles beneath turned from pink to brown and sizzled on the bones that carried them...all before he hit the floor.

Minutes later, Arnold opened the front door, whistling. He stepped over Fred's scorched body, walked over to the metal box, opened the door with the remote control, and removed Whiskers, who purred and licked his petting hands.

He looked down at the steaming body at his feet. "Can't beat home cookin', right Whiskers?" He sat down on the floor, picked a piece of meat off Fred's bones, blew on it, and fed it to the purring cat, who winced from the heat, but then gratefully chomped down.

CHOPPERS

She's so angry with me, the scissors buttermelt from the friction when I cut her hair. She fruitchecks my cheek and hostage negotiates the soggy clippers out of my hand. Later, she butters my toast with the molten blades and with a cupped palm under the mess babyfoods me the burnt bread. When I awaken and try to goodmorning her, something razorshaves inside my guts whenever I try to speak. My throat guitarstrings with a snap. So I go harpo and smile, silent, all hers, honking my horn while she cousinits me, her hair growing so long she eventually can braid it with her toes. It's almost long enough to lynch her from the ceiling and towelsnap her spine. But I feel her hands all gyno inside me now, molding new handles to fit her twitching fingers.

Amputating the Phantom

I chop off his arms.

His eyes swim around like ball bearings but then focus in. He just glares at me. Hard. It's that same look he used to get when he beat me: the look of death, desired. Each eye a cold glaze of dilated black pupil ensnared in a mesh of yellowed whites and bright red veins spider-webbing around in some perverse Easter egg design. His muscles clenched with the intensity of the torturer, nostrils flared, his complete sensorium absorbing as much of his victim's pain as it can.

I've turned him into a writhing little creature with no arms.

Yet he's still abusing me. Still draining my soul. Right now. With just that look, that glare, that absorption of my guilt.

Then I feel the air whirl between us and then there's a pool of pain on my face, a slash in my back, and fingertips sinking into my thighs. He's clawing at me with his phantom hands, beating me with his aura. I can see it in his eyes.

I bat away at the limbs before I move to chop again at the neck, wondering if this will ever stop, wondering if I have a phantom self who is cowering in pain and dying away even as I swing the blade.

How to Put a Cat to Sleep

First, you never actually use the words "sleep" or "death." You circumvent them. You avoid eye contact and point at charts and x-rays. You try to sell a little bit of hope, but you let the illuminated plastic film contradict your words. The lungs are half full of tumorous growth. The couple standing there can see the balloon inside her airway, just waiting to burst. You tap it with a pen to point out the obvious, but the action speaks louder than your words. And even more than this gesture, they can hear their pet's clotted pants and they can still feel the moist blood she'd coughed up, slick between their fingers from all the petting they're doing.

Next, you let them ask. Is it time? Should we do it? Please give it to us straight: what are her chances?

Some things you have to figure out as you go along. That's the part you hate most.

So you spill the beans in numbers and percentages. You give them your trusty anecdote about a dog named Buttercup who lived years after a similar diagnosis; you then mention Petunia, who surprised you by croaking in your arms when you put the thermometer up her bum. You let them ask questions, but you mostly let them come up with their own answers.

You leave them in the emergency room to talk to their cat while you and your assistant go into the hidden recesses of the clinic. Your assistants uncomfortably wipe old test tubes and organize charts. You risk eye contact and that confirms it: they're gonna do it. You fetch the poison and prep the anesthesia. Your main assistant grabs the tissue box and rubber gloves.

When you return, the tears say it all. But you ask what they want to do anyway, because it isn't really you that's killing the cat, it's them, and you want them to know that. The husband assents and the wife just nods and loses whatever she was holding back, pouring it into the cat with a hug. You explain the procedure and ask if there are any questions. There aren't any that you can answer.

You slide the blue needle in. To numb. Then the red one. To nod her off.

The cat blinks at the couple one last time. Slowly.

Eyes freeze half-open. The couple frowns in an unfathomable way.

You just nod and clench your teeth and balance your objective features against your empathetic eyes. When you withdraw the needle, blood leaks out in a way that only a dead body leaks it. You cover this up with cotton, but they see it.

Finally, you express your sympathies by reciting a Hallmark and then let the assistants explain the disposal and billing options.

As you return to your desk you realize that you've still got the red needle in your grip. There's still a little liquid unplunged, like hope.

Nightmare Job #3

WANTED: Town Sewage Treatment is now hiring expert diver for plant tanks. Must be willing to work nights and weekends. Must be willing to swim in the shit of a hundred thousand assholes. Responsibilities include: unclogging filtration systems by hand, manually replacing submerged mechanical parts, and maintaining chemical levels in sewage recycling. Bachelor's Degree in Chemistry at minimum required at time of employment. Organic Chemistry degree or Ph.D. in English a plus. Benefits include medical plan with low deductible, free diving suit with harpoon gun, and personal shower on premises. Town Sewage is an equal opportunity employer.

WHILE KNITTING YOUR HAT

She knits. You're examining a skein of her wool, wondering what color it's called, when she asks:

—Ever wonder what they did with all those baskets?

—Baskets?

—Those guillotine baskets…the ones they used to catch the head after it was chopped off.

—Oh.

She knits. The needlework sounds like blade sharpening. You say:

—No. I never thought of it.

She knits, pulling a woolen string.

—I mean, those were some pretty nice baskets. Had to be strong enough to hold a head.

You frown.

—They've gotta be around somewhere. I mean, those are some fine baskets. Someone must have kept them. Someone could use them for something.

She knits as your eyebrows pull down to match your frown.

—Maybe not the executioner or the guards, but maybe some peasant woman in the crowd. Maybe some woman like me who just needed a basket for her wool.

You look up at her with a determined roll of your eyes:

—I guess it's possible.

She reaches into your basket and—picking up the hat she's been knitting all along and sliding it down your temple—tries it on for size.

—How's that feel?

Itchy. But you say:

—Can you make it cover my ears? I'm so cold.

She smiles but it doesn't warm you up.

DISGRUNTLED

It's Casual Day in the office and Josh steals away a spare moment to dream.

He dreams of hunting down his office mates.

One by one, he picks them off with the rifle he imagines extends from the barrel of his line of sight. It's a heavy gun—its gravity pulls his head down with its weight. He spots Kimberly down the hall, carrying a stack of papers. A cartoon burst of color and light blinds him when he blinks and then she becomes a shower of manila files and blood smears on the wall. No more color coding for anyone on this floor—it's all red now.

More mindless robots pop their gaskets as he picks them off. Jules, bullet-ridden. Fredo, forgotten. Marcus, a stain.

Josh drops a pencil and sneaks a peek below the desk line, hoping to take any remaining drones out by their ankles. No foot knuckles to be seen. Wait: there crawls Desiree, the coffee machine junkie, on all fours. She must think Josh can't see her down below the desks. What's she doing there? Hiding? Looking for her contacts? She turns and faces him, a curl of brown hair spilling sexily down her cheek. She grins. The return of her gaze is so penetrating he feels like he's been hit.

Josh clutches his chest, tumbles to one shoulder.

Desiree laughs conspiratorially.

Josh doesn't bite, climbing back up to his chair and getting back to work. Typewriters and copy machines hum and clack.

Casual Day is sometimes more work than it seems.

On his way home, he imagines cop cars and ambulances rushing past him to charge into his office building. He can smell the tear gas canisters and the sweaty Kevlar of the SWAT teams. But it's a clean getaway.

Come Monday, he'll pretend that he returns to an empty building. They'll all be gone, victims of his secret rampage. The janitors will have mopped up most of it, but Josh will know where to look for secret traces of his crime.

Monday, he'll be the boss of the entire company. It'll be Casual Day forever.

If not, it'll be business as usual. But one thing will be different. He'll see their wounds when they walk by. Sharon, scarred. Harry, headless. Gregory, gimped.

They'll be worse than robotic employees. They'll be zombies back from the dead whose torsos and heads and limbs explode in a shower of red and yellow, all over again. They won't really be people at all. He'll be doing the world a favor.

Josh spends his off-time organizing ammunition and reviewing the inventory of his imaginary armory. Weekends, too, are sometimes more work than they seem.

Monday morning, alarms ring. Desiree brings him coffee. She's still laughing.

ANNIVERSARY MEAL

I dare to show her my forgetfulness: "What anniversary is this again?"

She plays with her food a little bit, refusing to look up at me from the dining table. The trappings of our romantic dinner seem to mock me. The room turns so quiet I can hear the flutter of the candelabra's flames and the subtle sigh in her flaring nostrils. She cuts meat and the knife squeaks awkwardly against bone. Then she rolls an eye up at me. Just one. "Sixth."

"Ah yes," I say before she sticks her tongue against her teeth to finish the word. "Number six."

Her one eye ogles me with exasperation as she chews.

I break eye contact to take a bite of my own meal. The meat is especially red and juicy, as if I were stabbing and slicing a soaked sponge.

It's hard to come up with something fresh to say after being together for so long. "I love you," I muster, looking quickly over her hardened facial features, "more than ever before."

She smiles. I see meat fibers caught between her teeth.

Six millennia. That's how long we've been together. The love of fresh marinated muscle never goes stale, but sometimes our conversation does. Especially when she doesn't mind her manners. So old, yet so uncultivated.

"The silverware isn't silver," I remind her as she clutches her knife.

She cuts another slice and together, for just a moment, we laugh.

Second Helping

At first glance, hell is a cliché—it's everything you expected. Black smoke and brimstone. Perverse demons delivering pain to burning bodies. Screams surround you, and that seems like the worst of it. But you feel unviolated. You walk barefoot on lukewarm coals, wondering when your own eternally mundane affliction will be served up.

You start to think boredom and banality is your punishment. But then you begin to notice original cruelties in the milieu.

A young man in a business suit sits in a prison of gold bars. Stacks of currency between his legs ignite whenever he touches them. Just outside his cell, a sunburned creature in leather teases him, hip cocked as she plays her whip on the floor, tapping a booted toe. She laughs every time his money goes up in flames, and then lashes him between the bars.

In another chamber, a woman's umbilicus spools out, fastened to a wheel spiked with handles. A chubby demon lethargically captains the wheel just an inch to the right before pulling a latch to hold it fast. He is unraveling her. You wonder why she doesn't crawl toward the man to loosen the tension on her tether, but then you realize she is chewing off her own limbs, pausing only to scream whenever he forwards the wheel one notch.

You imagine these terrible events are somehow ironically perfect—not simply bizarre afflictions to keep the devil entertained but somehow poetically just punishments. These souls are receiving just desserts. But since you don't know the victims, you aren't certain how or why.

Then you see the baby. She's trapped in a high chair, wailing.

A monster labors over the child with obese breasts leaking rivulets of lava from its nipples. What sin, you wonder, could a toddler possibly have committed to deserve this horrible place? And what cruel torture must this innocent girl bear?

As you approach, the baby pouts and refuses to eat what it's being force fed by the exasperated demon, who impatiently taps a spoon on its palm. You move closer and see that the spoon is a razor-edged ladle harboring blood in its bowl. The baby's mouth and cheeks are gored. Chunks of tissue suspend in a red rope dangling from its mouth. Its baby flesh is blotchy with strain. All its facial muscles clench, as if she's trying to squeeze more of the mouthy mess out of her head. But she's not holding her breath or grunting—she just shrieks like...

The screaming is too much to bear.

Here, you say, taking the spoon from the demon. Let me show you how I fed mine.

You blink and you're in the chair. The demon is thanking you. You stammer but your tongue is already falling out from the scoop she takes with the spoon. Your mouth overflows with liquid heat as she feeds the meat to your baby, who finally calms, and chews.

You begin to pout and refuse the next approach of the exasperated demon's tool.

Canines

My teeth hurt from chewing on bone. I go to see the dentist. He bites my neck to deaden the nerves.

Extracts.

They will grow back.

THE CURSE OF FAT FACE

The kids called her fat face. And when she looked in the mirror, she saw they were right: her cheeks were as thick as thighs, her eyes pushed in plump like buttons pinching back the fabric of her over-stuffed head.

She decided her face needed to diet. So she stopped feeding it attention.

She wore a scarf like a burka and hid behind sunglasses.

She avoided eye contact. Especially with mirrors.

She blinked. Often. She thought of this as a form of exercise, a way to melt away the cheek fat.

But mostly she just ground her teeth and did jaw exercises which required many private conversations with herself at night, alone in a dark bedroom.

All this was much to the consternation of her mother, who listened intently at the door, trying unsuccessfully to make out the language.

Miraculously, the fat-faced girl reached her goal in just three weeks. The kids began leaving her alone, targeting other people's faces for their assault of attention. Perhaps this was because she had become sallow and pale and scary.

Soon she found herself facially anorexic. Her button eyes now sank inside her cheeks like peach pits in empty pie pans. Her complexion waned; the black rings around her eyes triplicated concentrically. And her face fat was still there after all; she discovered it had moved to other parts of her skull, as if the cellulite had displaced to places where she'd pay more attention to it. It now hung in hammocks of flab from her jaw line and neck, like the dangly skin beneath an octogenarian's biceps.

At least, that's how the poor girl saw it. In her mother's eyes, she was simply thin.

A week later, her mother could take no more of her daughter's privacy and selfishness. She confronted her as she was gorging on Cosmo in the bathroom. The daughter confessed to spending sleepless nights with Vogue. She was bingeing on images of models between purges of attention, puking up pretty in ugly wet chunks. She knew she needed help and cried out to her mother.

But when they finally approached the hospital, racing in her mother's Cadillac, it was too late: Mother went over a speed bump and her daughter's fat face fell right off the bone, sloughing down from her earlobes and chin and slurping into her lap before spilling on the floor of her mother's fine luxury car.

Before they covered her with a sheet, Mother thought she looked impeccable, like perfect teeth polished to the color of clean whitewall tires. When she returned home, she scooped her daughter's remaining skin off the floor mats and poured it into a shiny jar to place on her mantel. Everyone who visited was mesmerized by their reflection within its grotesque beauty.

Fat Face returned their gazes, feeding, pressing up against the glass a little more tightly with every passing day.

SKULLDUGGERY

The boy without a skull decides one day to put aside the salad bowl he kept his head settled in. He dons a motorcycle helmet instead, and something about the new dimensions that enclose him feels free. Mother never understood—he needed to look cool. Absolutely *needed* to. And so he does, running away down the highway to find some new place where some new person will let him take it off once in awhile, even if it kills him.

CHANTING RICHARD

She chants his name over and over again: *Richard, Richard, Richard.* But in the maze of her mind her own voice echoes and reverberates and she hears another voice emerge from the cacophony, saying: *rich hurt, rich heard, rich heard, richer, dritcher...ditch.* Eventually she's singing "rich dirt" in the bass line and reaches for a shovel, knowing what she has to do.

The Eight Ball
in Big Mouth's Pocket

Jimmy Big Mouth and Jack "The Vacuum" Ohio were two of the biggest players to set chalk to stick at Nick's Side Pocket. I usually just ignored their legendary pool games while I sat at the bar, drinking my Miller and trying to forget about work in the waitress' eyes. But on the day Big Mouth challenged The Vacuum to a duel I'll never forget, I found myself holding my bladder and crossing my legs, just to catch a glimpse over the shoulders of a dozen other barflies to get a peek at Side Pocket history.

See, Big Mouth and The Vacuum were honorable hustlers, who split the pool hall's losers between them, even though they didn't work together. They made a ritual of playing a game of Eight Ball against each other at the end of every night, putting ten percent of their respective take up on the table. After twenty years of doing this, they were buddies, and the money wasn't anything more than a way of keeping score for them. The game was all a match of wits.

But on the night of their duel, Big Mouth had just a little too much to drink and decided to live up to his name and act like a smart ass. Apparently, during their last game of the night, he had The Vacuum snookered on his eight ball shot—the one which would have given him the game—and so Big Mouth thought he'd raise the stakes. "You make that shot," he said to The Vacuum, puffing on his trademark cigar, "and I'll eat that black ball like a sandwich."

Vacuum snickered, but it was one of those fake kinds that says a man is seriously angry. "Deal," he said too quick for argument, and shot so hard and fast you'd think his arm was the trigger of a big gun. The cue ball zipped across the felt lickety-split and smacked the eight ball with a sharp crack.

And the next thing you know, that black ball jumped off the table and sailed right into Big Mouth's face, knocking the cigar out from between his lips and lodging itself squarely between his yellow teeth when he'd opened his big mouth to scream. Big Mouth's eyes were as large as tractor tires, the number eight peeking out of his mouth like the pupil of some freak's giant glass eye.

"Welp," The Vacuum said walking over to him. "I scratched. You win." He grinned while he shoved Big Mouth's cut into his blazer jacket. "But Big Mouth, you know damned well that you weren't gonna leave this joint without eating that ball, either way." He slapped Big Mouth hard on the back and left the Side Pocket, cocky as could be.

None of the on-lookers—myself included—said a word. We watched in awe as Big Mouth turned his back to us, zipping his custom-made cue up in its black leather satchel. It was sad to see a man lose his pride that way, and to see the end of such a friendship between pros. Sure, Big Mouth had a big mouth, but he was still a role model to us all.

He didn't dare look us in the eyes as he slowly made his way out of the hall. He had a depressing look on his face—a homeless bulldog sort of mug—that almost made him look like a different person. When he got to the front door, he turned around to face us and broke the silence: "G'night boys," he said, chucking an eight ball to the bartender as if he'd just then spit it out. When I looked over at him, I couldn't help but notice that his face had brightened and he was smiling— freshly chipped tooth and all.

Well, Big Mouth didn't show up at the Side Pocket for a week or two, and many of us figured we'd never see him again. The Vacuum showed up nightly, of course, but he didn't get very much play from the regulars, who I reckon were afraid of him more than ashamed of being seen with the guy.

It was almost closing time one Friday night when Big Mouth finally returned to the pool hall for revenge. The entire joint—from bar to bathroom—turned silent as he approached The Vacuum. The Vacuum had a huge grin on his face, looking Big Mouth up and down as if he were just another loser off the street. "Guess who's hungry for more?" he asked nobody in particular.

Big Mouth nodded amicably, and withdrew a bankroll from his

blazer pocket, setting it on the green felt of the table. The Vacuum sneered at it, as if it were a roll of toilet paper.

"All that," Big Mouth said, motioning at the money, "and sole ownership of this hall. You win, I never step foot in this joint again. I win, you do likewise."

"You don't know when to quit, do ya?" Vacuum said, grabbing some chalk.

Big Mouth grabbed him by the wrist before he reached it. "Oh, and my bet still stands: loser eats the eight ball. Only fairly this time— after the ball sinks the pocket. Got it?"

The Vacuum's grin widened. "You sure must like the taste of ivory, fat man."

Big Mouth grinned right back at him, his front tooth chipped and gnarly.

Big Mouth racked them up while The Vacuum chalked his stick. By now, everyone in the joint had encircled the table to watch. No doubt about it: our little pool hall had been blessed with the biggest match in the history of billiards.

Both hustlers were dead serious in their play, not wasting any time with chit chat. The game was all that mattered, and the sticks flew quickly. The only sound in the hall was the crack of balls and the sigh of the crowd after each shot, missed or made.

In the end, Big Mouth had turned the tables on The Vacuum: the balls were set in much the same way they were when The Vacuum insulted him weeks ago, except Big Mouth had the advantage and it was his shot. He looked up at The Vacuum and winked. "Eight ball in the corner pocket," he said, ready to cinch the game.

The Vacuum grumbled. "No way, fatso. I've got you snookered."

Then Big Mouth made his move. He walked right over to the corner pocket, unzipped his pants, and lifted his butt cheeks right over the hole. He even had the audacity to pretend he was swallowing his stick like a sword as he grunted and amazingly squeezed an eight ball right out of his ass and into the pocket with a squishy thud.

No one gasped or laughed or looked away when Big Mouth sat up and zipped his pants. And no one in the crowd moved out of the way when The Vacuum tried to break through us to escape after Big Mouth said, "Now you eat it, ya bastard."

A Donation

I want to donate my body to science.

I want to soak in formaldehyde for a few years. I want to be cut up by practicing doctors, saviors of the future, then re-stitched, ready for the next class. I want to be probed and poked and pointed at. I want to be preserved. Why be buried or burned? Why frozen? I want my organs exposed.

And I want to be able to feel it. I want to be conscious when they lower me into a tank of preservative. I want to feel formaldehyde rushing into my eyes and ears. I want to feel it coursing down my throat. I want to feel it ballooning in my stomach and lungs. I want to feel puffy with eternal life.

And I want to teach. I want people to smell me. I want people to see me for what I am. I want people to get their hands wet when they dig inside me. I want people to laugh. I want people to gag. I want people to have nightmares. I want people to see my shriveled penis. I want people to be jealous. I want people to wonder where I am now. I want to see the looks on their faces as my skin is peeled back. I want to teach the unlearned. I want people to see what I really am, and could have been. I want people to see what they really are, and can be. And I want to live on, groping inside of them, just like they grope inside of me, searching for the truth.

Nightmare Job #4

You love your nasty job. Because it's easy. You are the hospital's "Biohazard Specialist," but all that means, mostly, is that you drive a truck from the hospital to the incinerator, delivering the disgusting stuff that no one else wants to think about, let alone look at. You carry Tupperware bowls filled with excised organs from the operating room to the truck virtually the same way the paramedics do with organ transplants, only this is the dead stuff, and you're the guy who is on the way out, not the way in. You're no hero, but you do your job just as efficiently. You forklift drums full of body liquids into your truck like construction workers do every day, working up a lot of under-appreciated sweat. And you load up the laundry service van with plastic bags full of linens heavy with bloodstains and soilure. It's no different than any hotel might do it. Only your bags are branded with those familiar four circles of the biohazard symbol.

That symbol might as well be from a Led Zeppelin album, if not for its blazing orange loudness. Still: you don't understand why this scares people away. Even from a distance, they avert their eyes, as if the symbol might blind them. You think it's kind of pretty.

You do your job well, and you even used to get paid well. But last year the hospital got hit with a huge malpractice settlement of some kind, just as the board had contracted for the installation of millions of dollars worth of fancy new machines. So your salary got cut. Not a lot. But enough to hurt a lot now, a year later.

Cut. Just like those body parts.

So when the strange man in the leather jacket offered to pay you on the sly for some of those Tupperware bins and bio bags, you obliged him. Why not? Who would know? Your whole job was about hiding the truth. The bigger the plastic tub, the more the man paid. You never asked any questions. The job never asked any questions. And he never asked any questions, either. Everyone was happy. And you finally got what you earned. No, you got more: enough to buy a fancy pair of sneakers.

Then the machinery came in. The stuff that incinerated the bits and pieces of bodies, and a special chemical dry-cleaning system for all fabrics. Suddenly they didn't need you anymore. You were demoted to janitor. The lesser title offered less pay.

You weren't about to sell your new white sneakers with the soft cushioned soles. You weren't about to take another pay cut. You weren't about to stop trading with the man in the leather coat.

You knew where to get the parts. You had a whole building at your disposal.

And the soiled laundry? Well, half of that would be your own.

HER DAILY BREAD

From her employer's porch, the Nanny cocked a pear-shaped ear to the sky. "Do you hear that sound, my little one? Our birds are calling for their food." She leaned forward and strapped the child into her stroller. The child's arms were a little chilled. "Do you think you'll need a jacket?"

The child made a face like a frown before tossing an arm forward to point its pudgy bare arm at the Nanny's face and giggle in response.

The Nanny returned a knowing grin and then grabbed her old denim bread bag, swinging the strap over her shoulders and clutching it like a purse. A bird whistled from afar. She left the child's jacket behind her. "No time. We must hurry to feed them now."

Together they went to the park. On the way, they passed a bakery which smelled of fresh bread and pastries. It was busier than usual: preparations were in order for Thanksgiving. The odor of yeast in the air was as pungent as old beer.

The child's pacifier spilled out of her mouth and onto the ground, and she began to sniffle and cry as the Nanny rolled the stroller into the center of the park, where an odd statue of a bald man on a throne sat thinking. The man in the statue reminded her of her husband, who had died in the war while the Nanny was pregnant. He was always thinking, always worrying, always concrete and still. The child bellowed. The Nanny slipped a tiny square of hard, dried bread into the child's tiny mouth to silence her. The child sucked on the brick in her mouth and bit, her gums scabbed and bleeding.

The Nanny found a bench for them. She could still smell bread, and that was one reason why the birds came: if the world was their home, this was their kitchen, and dinner was served. Turtledoves, charcoal gray and sharp beaked, always swarmed together in one big flock like a tightly-knit family clustering round the concrete table, ready to eat. One day the Nanny had seen all of them resting on the statue, covering its entire body like a large coat of feathers, or a living down blanket of tiny eyes, warming the soul of the body inside the concrete case. Her husband, she imagined, would be comfortable nestling inside such a coat.

The Nanny poked another square brick of bread into the child's mouth. And then another.

She dreamed about the child she had lost shortly after the letter came.

And the children she now fed. The ones who always flew away but always came back. She was their Nanny, too, bringing square worms of hard bread to them, daily. These birds, her children, would often skittle around the cobblestone walkways that surrounded the statue, chasing strangers with their beaks, pecking stones and pebbles which they mistakenly assumed were food. But when Nanny came they would cuddle and coo, patiently awaiting homemade croutons from the bag that rested atop her breast. They knew she would feed them.

The child tried to unclasp the belts that held her in the stroller like an automobile seat. The Nanny ignored her, slipping more bread into her mouth. Forcing it. The child cried out, but the sound was muffled by the gooey chunks of hard dough which clogged her mouth like clay mud and gravel. The birds were moving toward her now, pecking their way across the stones. The tapping of their talons, the Nanny thought, made the sound of water dripping into a basin. Like rain. Or tiny bullets. The flock encircled the child's stroller, waiting. Together they shared coos of approval.

The Nanny grinned. Her family was welcoming her home.

She tossed a handful of breadcrumbs over beside the statue's booted feet. The birds swarmed, taking flight, each trying to be the first to get the best bite. Some pecked each other—such squabbles were common in a close family. And she knew how hungry they could be so late in autumn. One time, the Nanny had tossed an entire plastic bag full of bread crumbs onto the cobblestone, and that had caused quite a stir: one bird was so badly wounded by the others that it had lost its wing.

The Nanny tossed another handful of stuffing beside a nearby bench. And again, the birds swarmed in a mad fury of feathers. They were hungry today. She was late.

The child's eyes were wide as oil puddles. Her muscles were as tightly locked as the statue's. She was bright pink. She frowned as she tried to press the bread out of her mouth with her tongue, but she was too busy choking on the mass, too busy trying to pull in air through small flaring nostrils.

And the Nanny continued to stuff her, thinking about another Thanksgiving without her husband. Without a child of her own. Alone with the yeasty smell of bread.

The child managed to break out of the straps around her chest, slipping down out of the stroller, cheeks puffed out like a billows. The Nanny did not notice—she was staring at the statue, her eyes dead and black, her hands mechanically plucking squares of bread out of her bag and dropping them into the sunken denim seat of the stroller.

The child ran for the statue. Searched madly for air.

And the birds swarmed in a flurry before covering her up in their gray autumn coat.

My Wound Still Weeps

They try to tell me I'm here because I have an eating disorder, but that's not it at all: it is not my stomach, but my wound that is perpetually empty.

It's on my left arm, a circular hole, wet and wide open, waiting for pink skin to sponge inside and fill it all up. It's right in the crook of my elbow—the spot where nurses draw blood—and that's why they've said it won't heal: because I don't hold my arm still. Especially when I'm eating—too much, too fast—so they've tried to change my habits, making me eat with a fork in my right hand or strapping my wrist to my thigh, instead. But that doesn't work at all. My wound still weeps. And I still eat to fill it up.

My wound is like a mutant eye—an eye that never shuts because the lids aren't long enough. And it cries. My wound weeps dark yellow tears that trickle warm down my forearm like the splash of spilled coffee.

It's been crying for years: outliving even Dad and his damned cigars. Sure, the cigars killed him, but that doesn't change what he did to me. He's dead of cancer, but he didn't lose anything: cancer is something that filled him up. It occupied him, flooded him up with black phlegm. Those cigars may have suffocated him, but he died full. Full of himself.

But me: my wound is on the outside. My hole won't ever fill. I can't feel it anymore—there's nothing there to feel. All I feel is perpetual leaking. And I've been losing a tiny bit of myself ever since.

So I eat.

Otherwise, the only thing I have to hold on to is that last moment—right before I started losing myself, drop by drop. I was being a brat, not finishing supper, and Dad was so mad at me because he had made the dinner himself with his very last dime. I don't remember what he cooked. But I do remember that it tasted horrible and that I couldn't swallow anymore. When he said I had to, it was all we could afford, I asked him how he paid for his cigars. I can still feel the pain from when Dad slammed my wrist down on the kitchen table and gently rested his hot heavy cigar on the soft white underside of my elbow, the fat roll of tobacco stoking on my arm as if in a ceramic ashtray. What got me worse than the bright red pain was the smell of his cigar smoke, somehow made more potent with the catalyst of my flesh to smolder. I cried, I begged him to put the cigar out, and after I finally promised to finish my dinner, he did, lifting my wrist up to my shoulder, squelching the hot coal between the chub of my forearm and biceps. I think it was then that I dropped the fork I had been squeezing for my life. And when he let go of me, I kept my arm bent, holding the cigar in place like gripping the gauze the nurse gives you after taking blood: grasping the pain like a plug in your elbow—flexing your muscles so you won't empty out through the puncture.

But that's all I've been doing for years. Emptying out.

I know I eat too much, more than my stomach can hold, but I never gain weight: I just keep on leaking. My wound sometimes closes, but it never stays shut—always stretching itself open to spill more coffee tears, always widening just a little bit further, always peeling its eyelid back when I sleep. Sometimes the white fibers of tendon peek out from their sticky blanket of yellow, crusted like an eye waking up in the morning beside me.

It won't fill me up, but still I keep eating.

Because when I don't, sometimes I catch it out of the corner of my eye: a tiny tuft of gray smoke, rising up from my elbow.

Peeling the scabs with my teeth, I'm really just trying to feed it itself. That's what they don't understand. There's a chance that if I keep eating, my wound might stop weeping. I know what it's like when smoke gets in your eyes. Crying over dinner. Tasting tears. But I won't break my promise: *yes, Dad, I will finish.*

THE BLOOD RAN OUT

The blood ran out from the ungourmet gash, the usual gnawed neck, the unpretty wound. It streamed, ran, hurried as if each drop was fleeing from his dry green tongue for the sanctuary of soil beneath the body—first fast then madly escaping as the heart inside his victim thrashed its mighty self for survival—then slow, too slow as it trickled, dribbled, gave up—and as he lapped he tried not to look, he tried not to see, tried not to forget the memory of himself long ago as he tearlessly cried and died the first time. He clenched his eyes tight to bring stars of new blood to his eternal inner night. He fingered his victim's wound gingerly, spreading its rough edges like sticky chapped lips for a kiss, then brought the wet tip of his finger to his own neck, lubricating the ancient cut, feeling the similar wound there— almost alive as he swallowed—reading the Braille of his flesh bitten long ago for the imprinted memory there of his first time when...

the blood ran out from his neck and he couldn't stop it no matter how hard he struggled with the thing chewing into his voice box—the ever-crunching jaws biting through his shaking fingers, his palms, his wrists...everything he had to try to stop the bleeding and the thing that sucked sucked his life away, his life away into this new imitation of life with the first dusk, believing he had awakened from a terrible daydream, then remembering the struggle with death's darkness, imagining this might be heaven after all until the hunger, hunger in not so much his stomach but his soul sucked so far inside-out that now he was the swirling vortex of confusion, now he was the one who sucked, took, fed on nature's fluid return, becoming not life but a living hunger, a hunger, hungry...

the blood ran out from between his lips, he was choking on it, choking on his memories too, pressing his wound and trying to swallow life too fast—and he quickly realized that others had gathered around him—at least ten hungry souls just like him—crowding out his peaceful memories with their incessant quest for food—wrestling with limbs, writhing naked in the soil around him as they fought over his kill— starving animals trying to yank even him out of the way with their mouths and sharp fingers, as if he could feel pain—their voices growling in the dark as they fed on the remnants of the dissipating soul he'd swallowed—their gleaming green mouths snarling and thrashing on the flesh he'd already nearly emptied himself. Again he tearlessly cried as the others parasited his kill—licking the bottom of this barrel of flesh he had already drained. These others weren't just stealing his meat—they were stealing a part of him, what little he had and was, too. They were all so hungry. And he could sense others out there in the night, rushing toward this empty field where he had minutes ago happened upon the first real human he'd seen in months, at first thinking the smell of fresh sweat and the hot thump thumping he felt in the distance were merely figments of his imagination, a mirage of a meal in the hunger of his empty void that had sucked so long on nothing but darkness that he had taken to animals and insects and even they were hard to come by anymore and so he pounced on his imagi- nary human feast like a dreamer rapes a pillow in dreams—because he needs to know if it's real—if he's real—but this time he was not the only one dreaming of food—far from it—there was nothing anymore but crying lost and empty hungry souls around him—a nauseating universe of dizzy dark mirrors—and he was so surprised that this one lunging and desperate bite hit home—that his imaginary vision was real—that his teeth had sunken into real flesh, real blood, and as his hunger subsided to pulsing satisfaction he did not stop the gluttony he did not stop to rest he did not stop feeding as the others tore free his limbs—then his torso—to make room for their orgy of snouts and...

the blood ran out from the back of his throat—tongues reaming the open hole on the underside of his gutted neck. He knew full well he was decapitated but still eating, chewing, biting, teeth clamped on the body to hold on—a vortex feeding the other vortices—an ever-open mouth feeding other mouths—sucking sucking sucking as the blood ran out ran out ran out—because he knew—as did the growing mountain of others chewing their way into the back of his brain—that this could be the last time for all of them—and as he himself was eaten he ate he ate he ate because this could very well be the night...

the blood ran out for good.

An Evil Eye

It sits in a dish on my desk in a puddle of pink jelly. The eye is blue and trails the surprisingly yellow and white fibers of optic nerve behind it. There's a glazed look about it—and a flatness to its shape that is very unappealing. I wonder whether it leaks optic fluid, or has decompressed now that it has been freed from its imprisoning socket.

The worst part about this evil eye is that it refuses to look at me, no matter how confrontationally I position it. I cannot see myself through it and wonder if I ever did. My remaining eye finds its former partner in crime a complete stranger. And it wonders what this stranger is doing whenever it blinks.

Hand in Marriage

The dismembered finger quivers in a puddle of its own blood. Although it bears some prints, the ring snugly wrapped below the second knuckle is a clue he cannot leave behind. He slides it free and slips it on his own ring finger, right above the white lines where his own wedding band used to be. No one will ever know how much he loved her. This almost feels the same.

PHRENOLOGICAL LOVE

"Stop that, Mark! It tickles!"

Ah, and it tickled me, too. Tickled me pink. It isn't often that I get to dig my fingers into a beautiful woman's hair, feeling the taut nap of her scalp and the smooth fissures of her skull. And because it was Roxy, I was all the more excited.

Roxy was going steady with Bud, my best friend. I'd always been attracted to Roxy...something about the way her face was shaped—a semi-oval disk of a head, with strong, sharp cheeks, all surrounded by wondrous tresses of blond—had always driven me to stare at her, blushing (especially when Bud was around). I wondered what it would be like to touch her, to inhale her perfume, to kiss her, to hold her. But it was truly the shape of her head that pulled me toward her like a magnet, and now, finally, I had the chance to discover just what it was about that bone structure that enchanted me so.

Of course, I'd never voice my opinions to Roxy. Not even now. After all, it was Bud's idea for us to get together in my dorm room like this in the first place. He had suggested that I give Roxy a phrenological exam, to possibly help her in choosing a major. He couldn't be there for the whole affair because of football practice, and I didn't have time until nightfall, because of my work-study duties. So when Roxy came over—alone—shortly after dusk, I couldn't help but think of it as a date. I couldn't express my emotions to Roxy, but still, I caressed her scalp like a lover.

The vibration of her voice through my fingertips interrupted my concentration: "Where'd you pick up all this phrenology nonsense anyway? I thought this sort of thing went out long before Freud."

I sighed. "It's still around, though no one takes it as seriously as I do." I continued to seek out the lumps and fissures of her skull with my fingertips, being careful not to pull her soft, wonderful hair. "I found a book on phrenology in the library a long time ago, and have been practicing it ever since. What impressed me the most was how scientific it all was. It's not like palm reading or tarot cards, you know. Every inch of scalp tells something about the mental functions of the person in detail, and my diagnoses haven't been wrong yet!"

"I seriously doubt that."

"It's true. Bud recommended me to you tonight because I helped him so much! The large lump over Bud's right ear told me that although he has a strong intellect, he was mentally suppressing his athletic abilities. It was because of my phrenology that he joined the football team two years ago, and look at him today: first string quarterback, on a full ride scholarship!"

Her eyes rolled up to look at me, and I avoided their magnetic, cobalt blue. "And what does my scalp tell you?"

"I can't tell, you keep moving. Hold still."

She obeyed.

My living room was silent, save for the slight wispy sound of my probing fingers, rambling like spiders amid the blond shafts of her hair. I found it difficult to concentrate—not because she kept moving, but because she was there at all. Especially right there between my legs, with her back to me, sitting on the floor Indian style while I sat above her on the couch. To an outside observer, we might have looked like two lovers returned from a recent campout, checking one another's scalps for ticks.

But without Bud being there to watch, I felt more like a rapist than a lover, stealing these little moments of pleasure from Roxy, violating her without her knowledge.

And when I realized this, I began to lie. As I trailed my fingernail across a long fissure, I told her that it meant she would live a long life. I kneaded a small lump above her cerebrum, mentioning that she was probably an over-achiever at both work and play. I stroked a cavern above her left temple, and could not hold back the words that spilled from my lips like water from a drowning man...

That she would probably be better off if she stayed away from Bud, that the crevice in her skull was symbolic of how empty their relationship was, how devoid her life was of the love and happiness and pleasure that she really desired, and *deserved*, and that Bud was no good in bed, that he couldn't satisfy her, and that that was perhaps the biggest shame of all...

She snapped her head from my hands and leapt up, and as the shock of what I had done slowly subsided and reality returned, I realized that my fist was full of a surprising amount of her hair. I expected to hear the slam of my front door.

But she did not leave. When I finally built up enough courage to look up, Roxy stood above me, arms crossed, head cocked to one side, admonishing me. It was more than just the hair-pulling that accounted for her pained expression. "What the hell do you think you're doing?" Her eyes bore into mine like shards of jagged blue glass.

I shrugged. I was not ready to admit, nor deny my guilt.

"Bud said that you might be able to help me pick a major, and that's all." Confusion swarmed her expression. "I'm not sure I want to hear all that other stuff."

The wavering sound of her voice was not anger. It was a cue: I had managed to accidentally push a button—a soft spot, if you will—that had set off a chain reaction of interior emotions. I wasn't sure exactly what I had said that smacked of truth, but it was something.

And the look in her eyes told me she wanted more of the same.

I hid behind the old stand-by: "I only reveal what's already there, in the lumps and bumps of your skull. I only speak the truth."

She cocked her head to the other side, pondering my clichéd and Gypsy-like reply. Couldn't she tell by the way I blushed, by the way my eyes pleaded with her, by the way I had caressed her skull only moments ago that the real truth behind my lies was that I wanted her?

Apparently not. She was too overwhelmed by the prospect of getting to know herself better from my phrenological probes to pay attention to me and my deep feelings. It was with a certain bitterness that I had only then realized her colossal egocentricity. Perhaps this was why Bud had tried to avoid her at times…because she was so downright selfish?

Her muscles loosened as she relaxed, and, sighing, she sauntered back to the sofa to sit next to me. She was going to give me a second chance, and from her expression I could tell that she thought I should consider it a privilege and an honor.

She grunted: "Oh, your couch is so uncomfortable. You really should get your cushions restuffed." She shuffled around, trying to find a more suitable position, and then faced me. "Okay, so tell me more." She looked at me, her eyes pouring out the attentiveness of a school child.

"Well, I'd have to go over you one more time to be sure, but like I said you're likely to live a long life. I can tell because—generally speaking, of course—your entire cranium is compact and with few major contusions, or bumps. This means that your brain has an enormous capacity for handling stress. This data, combined with the strength of certain physiogenic fissures lead me to believe that you are an over-achiever at work and play, and as far as I know, this is true…"

"Cut the bullshit."

"It's true!" It wasn't, but the art of persuasion can sometimes seem truer to life than any of us can explain.

"No, it's not that those things aren't interesting. Sure they are." She twisted in the couch, bringing one of her legs up and tucking it under the other, resting her arm across the sofa's back as if she wanted to cuddle with me.

I nervously coughed, and avoided her eyes.

"But what I want to really know about is those things you said about Bud. It's all true. How could you know such things?"

So that was the button I had pressed.

She continued: "We've really been on the skids lately. I hardly ever see him because of football practice. And we hardly, uh, you know…make love…because of football, too. My homework is suffering…I'm suffering, because of it all. I want to know what to do to fix things."

I stroked my chin, feigning wisdom. "Get rid of him."

The room was silent as she contemplated the thought. Then she said, softly: "But I need him."

I forced myself to look at her. "Do you? Do you really need to put up with all that he's done to you? Ignoring you every day, expecting you to be at his beck and call?"

"It's not like that!"

"Well, maybe it is, and maybe it isn't. But something is wrong with your love life." I put on my best smile. "Your head reads like a bad romance novel."

She raised an eyebrow. "You wouldn't be saying all this just to break me and Bud up, would you?"

She had me pinned. That was exactly what I wanted to do and she knew it. Being exposed as such, I was more nervous than I'd ever been in my life. I mentally suppressed the thunder pounding in my chest, which seemed to echo against the walls of my room. A trickle of sweat ran down my right cheek. I couldn't help but say, "Ye..." when she cut me off:

"Because if this is Bud's sick way of dumping me—getting you to break the news to me with all this mumbo-jumbo, I'll kill the bastard."

I relaxed, leaning back against the cushions of my couch. "Don't you see the hostility you have for him? Can't you hear it in your own voice? You two don't belong together. Not because he's playing some prank on you. I really did get all my information from your skull— phrenology really is my hobby, and I'm quite good at it. If anything, though, Bud is in love with you, desperately. I break this truth to you to spare him from the same pain that you are feeling, because in the end he would be devastated if you lead him on any longer, only for your relationship to come to its inevitable conclusion. He'd be crushed, and so would you. Break up now, before it's too late!"

Lies. All of it.

"Do you really think so? You aren't making more out of my head than what's there, are you?"

"Of course not!" Another lie.

She let it all sink in, and then she flashed a smile at me. "I believe you. How couldn't I? You obviously know what you're doing...and I think you really do care about Bud, don't you?"

"Of course I do. I wouldn't have said anything if I didn't care."

Her eyes gleamed a darker blue. "And you care about me, too, don't you?"

Before I had the chance to blush the brightest shade of pink and scream YES, she moved. Poetically smooth and graceful, with the perfect speed of true desire, her lips pressed against my own, moist and soft. We kissed and held each other for a long time, feeling and probing for lumps other than the ones that are found on heads.

Soon she pulled away, and her eyes gleamed, her pupils so dilated I felt I could fall down into them. But then she knotted her brow up into a question mark of confusion, as if all this was happening too fast. Perhaps it was, but I would have killed her if she would have thrown out the line, "Not tonight, I have a headache." From the look on her face, that was exactly the gist of what she was about to tell me. I was to be rejected.

She must have noticed my frown, because she suddenly said,

"Hey, I just thought of something!" Before I could stop her, she bounced onto the floor, resuming her position from earlier. "Read my head again; see what it says about you and me. Our relationship. Will it work?"

I hesitated. I had not yet truly felt her cranium in the phrenological sense...all my words thus far had been lies. Distracted by her presence and focused on my lies, I had only a partial glimpse of what she was really like from my reading so far, only a snippet of what mental secrets were hidden beneath her wondrous tresses of blond like buried treasure. And I wasn't sure I really wanted to know anymore, either.

I slid my fingers again into the thatch of beautiful hair, and immediately discovered the protrusion in her skull that I knew would be there.

She interrupted me, but I hardly paid attention: "And you still haven't told me which major I should pick yet, either..."

I caressed the lump that I wished was not there. Gingerly, I spread the hairs away from it, revealing the tip of this tiny mountain of bone that poisoned the lovely topographical map of her scalp.

It was the Zone of Ego—the area of the cranium that reveals the amount of egomania and selfishness in the subject—and Roxy's was unnaturally large. Monstrously huge. As outrageously gigantic as a rhino's horn, hidden in plain sight all along.

"...and don't go making more out of me than what's there again, either. You think I didn't know that you had a crush on me since we first met? A girl like me can tell such things..."

Her words faded from my conscious. All I heard her say was something about making more out of her. From the size of that horrid lump, I'd be hard pressed to think that there could be more!

But less...

"I think I love you," I said, slipping a free hand underneath the cushion of my sofa, finding the object that made her uncomfortable earlier, when she sat on it.

"What's there not to love?" she replied, oh so perfectly.

I brought the mallet down hard. "In a couple minutes, I'll explain it to you."

It took longer than that, though, for new lumps and bumps kept rising with each crack of the hammer. I couldn't find one worth having.

Roxy was better off flat.

THE CUT OF MY JIB

My jib only pops out once in a while. But it always embarrasses me. I'll be at work sipping coffee at my desk and then suddenly I'll feel the itchy tug between my shoulder blades and then—*pow*—a nub of white bone is sprouting from the flesh like the nose of a dolphin that's eaten me out from the inside. It hoists sail with a gurgle and I feel my innards catch wind as the organic wings crest above my cubicle.

My coworkers never fail to comment when my jib is flapping and I'm running against the wind. They tell me they like the cut of my jib, but I can see in their eyes they're threatened by my flesh flag beating taut against my mast of spine, its wet ropes of tendon spraying a pink mist of plasma.

My jib keeps me from going with the flow. That's its whole purpose. I can't stop it. It's my automatic resistance system. And my bosses don't like that, either. When my jib breaches my back during staff meetings, the higher-ups reveal the secret face of repulsion they make in bathroom stalls. If I sail into the lunchroom full mast, the chit-chat stops and my coworkers clutch their knives.

Sometimes my jib retracts. That's just as embarrassing.

Those who know about sailing know I could lower the boom at any moment. They're the ones who usually climb aboard. And I carry them through the day on a course uncharted. They cuddle in my hull and marvel at the sky. And though I keep steady watch from this eagle's nest skull through the binoculars of my eyes, the wind takes us where it will.

Sometimes it takes us on vacation. Other times, we're on the attack, charging those robotic motor boats of the office like pirates swinging on ropes with rusty knives clamped between our jaws.

And sometimes I just sit on the rooftop and brood with the gargoyles, wondering if this is where I belong or if my sails were built in to send me elsewhere.

THE LEAF PILE

Leaves fall around my shoulders as I rake over the dead past, drinking and doing a little yard work with my wife beneath a tall cedar. The leaves tumble-twist drunkenly around me like confetti party favors and I stop to toast her with my flask.

She refuses to drink with me.

I pocket the decanter, but stumble into the over-stuffed black plastic bag at my feet, spilling its contents and undoing all my hard work. Spinning sideways I catch myself almost stepping on the comb of my rake beside the leaf pile. She's there, laughing, and suddenly reaches up from the mound to pull me down with her. We wrestle in the musky pillow of leaves, shoving the cold foliage down the necks of coats and the waists of beltlines, rustling bunches of brown around puffy red ears, blindly tossing giant handfuls of the stuff in the direction of giggling voices as we struggle to get our bearings.

Gaining an advantage, I pin her down in the slick pile beneath us, the toes of my feet sliding as we stare at one another and breathe fog into our faces and smile as we catch each other's breath and almost kiss before she quickly rolls away from me, swishing under the leaves, and I twist and squirm to find her in this sprawl of fallen foliage only to bump my head on her tombstone.

The rake by my feet looks a lot like a shovel.

Dizzy, I madly scrabble around until I have to cry uncle, hugging the emptied black plastic bag to my chest, begging her to stop torturing me with leaves, to stop teasing me with her laughter, to stop hiding in that godforsaken pile.

Receiver

4:30pm

"Hi there, you've reached 549-2001. Sorry, but I'm not home right now. If you'd just leave your message at the sound of the tone, I'll get back to you as soon as possible."

Beep.

"Uh, hi, Julie. Jack here. Just calling to let you know that I won't be able to pick you up at home. Bob said that he has to talk to me before we go. He says it's urgent, but he won't be able to get off work until six. Since our plane leaves at eight, I think it'll be better if I just meet you at the airport. Take a taxi. I promise to pay you back.

"I still can't believe that we're really going to the Bahamas! It's gonna be great lying next to you on the sunny beach while Bob is gonna be stuck back here in the city, freezing his butt off on the way to work. See you around seven at the airport!"

Click.

6:24pm

Beep.

"Can you hear me, Julie? Pick up if you can. I'm at Bob's house right now. He can't hear me 'cause he's in the other room. Listen, we might have to cancel our flight. Bob says that the office just got a big order in, and they might need me to help out with all the paperwork. How dare they try to ruin my vacation! Anyway, things aren't sure yet, so I'll have to call back later. I hope you come home soon so I can talk to you instead of talking to myself! And don't you still have to pack? I'll call back in a half hour. Love ya."

Click.

7:08pm

Beep.

"Pick up, Julie. Pick up. Aren't you home yet? Listen closely 'cause I don't have much time to talk. I'm still at Bob's place. Things got a little out of hand here. He had a bit too much to drink and started running off at the mouth like he usually does after a few. I didn't know whether to believe him or not. He was talking all sorts of trash about you. Remember how he said that the office got a new order? He confessed to it all being a lie. He said that he purposely tried to stop me from going. And do you know why? He said that you two are lovers. He was probably just making it up, trying to live out his fantasies or something. But then he pulled a gun out on me to stop me from leaving. I couldn't help myself. I knocked him out. I know that what he said couldn't be true, otherwise you wouldn't be going to the Bahamas with me!

"Damn, time's-a-wasting. I can't believe I talked for so long. I guess I ramble at the mouth when I drink too much, too. I'm gonna sit here and wait for Bob to wake up so I can get the truth out of him. I'll beat it out of him if he doesn't come clean. After all, he's gotta realize that you aren't for sale. You're mine, Julie. Oh well, we'll see what happens. You better start packing! I'll try calling again later, before I leave for the airport, just to make sure that everything's okay. See ya!"

Click.

7:35pm

Beep.

"Oh Julie, will you please pick up the phone! I know you're there! C'mon!

"*We have to go right now!* I'm in big trouble here. Bob finally came to. I held his gun on him and he told me some pretty wild stories. He told me that he lied again. And this time I'm starting to believe him! He said that he killed you when he found out that you were going to the Bahamas with me. He said that you were cheating on *him*. He said that you were all his, not mine. He said that he was sorry, and begged me to take him to the cops and turn him in. But that wasn't good enough for me. I'm so stupid. I must be really drunk, 'cause I believed the things he was saying. After all, you haven't been home for the past one hundred times that I've tried to call you!

"I shot him, Julie. I killed Bob. It was an accident, I swear! I was just so damned drunk, and pissed, and sick of Bob's line of bull that I pulled the trigger.

"But I'm sober now. The sound of a gun going off in your own hand brings you back to reality real quick. Bob's dead, so we have to go *right now!* I know that you're still alive. I know Bob didn't kill you. He doesn't have the guts. And I don't believe a word that he said. So I'll meet you at the airport. Leave right away!"

Click.

7:58pm

Beep.

"Oh, Julie. Please, please, *please* pick up the phone. I know you're there. I know that you're alive.

"If you aren't there, I pray that you are on your way to the airport. I'm here waiting for you. Our plane leaves in two minutes.

If you really, really, really *are* dead, the cops are gonna pin it on me. They are already gonna pin Bob on me. But I don't care, 'cause I'll be out of the country and I'm never gonna come back. If you really *are* dead, then I didn't kill Bob in vain. I'll be glad that I did it.

"Please, honey, pick up the phone. If only just to say goodbye.

"Damn, they're announcing last call. I have to go. I'll never forget you, Julie. You were my life. But now I must go start another. Goodbye, Julie. I'll never forget you."

Click.

8:15pm

Beep.

"Julie: it worked! I told you that I could get you out of going to the Bahamas with Jack. But I did even better than that! I got rid of him for good. He's going to the Bahamas without you, and he's never coming back! Can you believe it? Sometimes I even impress myself. Those acting classes finally paid off. I probably couldn't have done it without the prop gun I stole from them.

"Anyway, now that Jack's out of the picture for good, how about coming over to your loving Bobby's arms? I know that you aren't gonna be home until late, making sure that Jack doesn't come over, but I'll wait up for you. I don't care how late it gets, come on over! I can't wait to hold you!

"I love you. Hopefully I'll see you soon. Bye-bye!"
Click.

Next day: 7:30am

Beep.

"What's the matter Julie? How come you haven't come over yet? I stayed up all night waiting for you! I bet you got a hotel room and slept there, huh? Well, call me as soon as possible. I'll leave my answering machine on. I've gotta go to work now. How about a romantic dinner tonight, or a play? I'll get back with you later. See ya!"
Click.

8:13am

Beep.

"Hi Bob! This is Julie. I'm shouting because I know that you probably can't hear me too good. It probably sounds like I'm a million miles away.

"Well, that's because I am. I took an early flight to the Bahamas. I'm sorry, Bob, I just couldn't break up with Jack. He's such a kind man. I don't know if I love him or not. Matter of fact, I don't know if I love you or not, either. That's why I left early. To make up my mind.

"You know what? I kind of like it here. It's peaceful. Maybe I'll stay here for good. I'm sick of being a secretary. Hell, I could be a beach bum my whole life! Maybe I'll find Jack; he should be here by now. Maybe I'll ask if he wants to stay here with me forever. I could live with that. Think he'll have any objections? Do you think he'll even be happy to see me, considering I left without telling him? We'll see.

"Sorry, Bob. I guess I just made up my mind. Goodbye forever. It was fun while it lasted."
Click.

SURGE

I was there the day the surgeon quit for good. He'd made an incision and accidentally set loose a really nasty vein. The spurting purple hose kept slithering out from between his slippery latexed fingers and glorping blood all over his fist. I thought he'd really done some damage and almost didn't hand him the clamp he demanded, but I knew there was no other way to stop the bleeding.

And all the while he kept saying, "She won't shut up…she won't shut up…she won't shut up."

A voice in his head? A memory? Did he know this patient personally? Or was his hearing so acute he could detect someone speaking nearby? Or perhaps I was misunderstanding altogether. I couldn't really hear well given that the heart monitor had flatlined.

But when he'd finished clamping the vein, it jumped back into its rhythm and everyone focused on keeping the patient's heart pumping. I alone realized that the surgeon had stopped his manic mantra.

He looked down at the sloppy pit in the patient's chest, breathing heavily. "Close," he commanded and slapped his wet palms together like a Vegas blackjack dealer. Then he rushed toward the operating doors as if chased.

As I reached for my suture, the vein pouted at me with two tightly pursed lips.

CONVICTIONS

Ah, finally, again, death. Again through the process of dying, this nightmare dream of bliss comforts me. It is better than any dream of returning to the womb. It is a journey to Heaven.

The darkness is cold, but I am not afraid. The Twenty-Third Psalm echoes in this endless corridor against walls unseen.

Maybe they aren't walls. Maybe they're bars.

I will fear no evil.

I walk forward, though there is no earth or floor to support my steps. Just the words of the Psalm. Am I walking? Am I still of the body?

I have been here before. Not only during sleep. The memory tries to take shape, but I won't let it. What does the past matter now?

Warmth suddenly seeps into my bones. Yes, I am still of the body. Something has to carry my soul forward to my destination now, doesn't it?

And now I can see. A pinhole of light in front of me, yet I am unable to judge how far ahead it is. The light must be source of the heat filling my bones. I must be close.

Thy rod and thy staff, they comfort me.

I reach out to touch the light, momentarily cutting it off. It's right in front of me!

It feels like a hole in some sort of wall. Must I dig my way out of this imprisoning cave of darkness? I struggle at its edges, which feel like metal.

And I bump into a round ball. A doorknob?

I twist. I pull. The light floods out around me, warmth turning to sweltering heat. A drop of sweat runs down the bridge of my nose. I am of the body, indeed.

I cannot see through the light, due to momentary blindness. Where am I? Have I reached my place in Heaven?

I step forward, shading my eyes. The door slams behind me. I am out of the darkness forever.

And then comes a sound! It is a fizzly hum, like a refrigerator's.

And with the hum comes the dimming of the light. I lower my hands to see.

A marvelous throne stands before me, empty. The throne of judgement? Some sort of carrier to the heavens?

The silence does not answer. The echoes of the Twenty-Third Psalm are gone.

But I am not afraid. I know that I have been here before. Familiarity comforts me. I know that I am safe. I know that I shall reach my destiny.

I sit in my humble throne, straining its wood with the sweat of my naked body.

The hum stops. The blinding light returns. And then shapes enter through the door. I cannot see what they look like. They are mere shadows and silhouettes.

One of the figures begins to change. *Yea, though I walk through the valley of the Shadow of Death…*

The psalm does not echo in this room.

"Who are you?" I beg toward the voice.

The chant continues. *I shall fear no evil.*

"But I'm already dead!"

The chant continues. I try to stand, but my arms and legs are locked in place. Shackles! Metal shackles! I shake my head and bump it on some sort of metal lampshade.

And then I remember. I remember it all, past and present.

I am sitting in an electric chair.

I sweat. I scream. I struggle for freedom. I hear the hum again, voltage building like a rising cobra, waiting for the right moment to strike.

A switch slams and then the light comes on. My wife is waking me, asking what is wrong. She tells me that it's just another nightmare and—exasperated—suggests again that it's time for therapy. When she says that, I hear "shock therapy." But still I tell her I just might. She lights a cigarette for me before falling back into her pillow.

I get out of bed to let her return to sleep's womb. I go to the kitchen to get a beer out of the humming refrigerator. I sit in the living room in my favorite chair and watch the sunrise service on Channel Seven.

After the sun breaks the horizon, stretching into my living room through a crack in the curtains, I finish my fifth beer and get ready for work.

I put on my uniform and head out to the prison, trying to recall if I've even told my wife that I've been working the row for the past month. The sunlight blinds me and I pull down the visor for shade as I drive.

VALENDINE

He buys plain pink sidewalk chalk and uses his used carving knife to carve the meaningless sticks into the meaningful shape of little pink hearts. He heartlessly etches valentine's etchings into every single one: Luv Ya, Kiss Me, Sweetie Pie. Then he inserts them into her lips, one by one as cautiously as a suicide sips suicide pills. He lines them up in her bloodied up gums side by side like thirty-two teeth in a tombstone smile. He kisses her lips then gnashes her jaws to make her chew up the dust of his lust to dust.

CONTUSED

I keep the right hand of my father in a wooden box, lined with purple velvet. The stump is capped with nickel plating, nailed directly into the bone. The flesh is bloated with embalming fluid, but quite supple where purple bruises are presently blotched. This leathery palm used to bruise me, instead. These swollen knuckles used to punch me bloody. But now the tables have turned. And I'm finding it hard to slap myself without ruining it. Even if I thump the plated end against my forehead, nothing stops the rotting inside.

Sinking Sandy

It's the perfect day for drowning, Sandy thinks, head drooping backwards on slim shoulder blades, neck craned up at the sun, legs crooked to air the knee pits, body poised like a deep brown insect sacrificing its carapace to sun. The ocean before her is deep blue and twinkling white—an irrelevant glare whose reflection warms her toes and knees and chin. She can feel its heat glimmering in the white gooey oil congealed on the underside of her breasts like a wiry bra of sunshine, wet with the decay of soon-to-be rust. No one is out here. She is nude and glowing and alone.

A perfect day for drowning. Later. Maybe when more people arrive to swim or surf or barbecue. Maybe when the sun throbs down in the water like a heart losing its pulse, its perfect disk infinitely hacked by the wafer thin serrated edge of the watery horizon: the butchering dusk. Maybe she'll convince herself not to drown at all, but she doesn't think it's likely. She's been through it all before—the volume of bellowing arguments inside her skull rising so quickly, so painfully, that it would always reach the point where she had to step outside and have a cigarette, leaning her back against the walls of her mind, feeling only the vibrations of grumbling voices inside but no longer making out their words—soon wandering off until she disappeared and ended up back…

Here on the beach, tanning her body. A futile gesture, she knew. But she wanted to go out in style. Maybe give the fisherman—a gray bearded man she imagined would reel her in on a hook intended for sharks—something to think about, maybe even give him a hard-on, maybe even make him spill his seed in the water before he rowed her ashore. Always good to think of rebirth, reincarnation—giving some-thing back, making it all worthwhile. It was the only thing she was sure of: her death would mean something—something she couldn't understand yet, and perhaps never would, but that something would inevitably happen with or without her choosing. That was the way nature worked.

The sand was getting hot beneath her towel and she flipped over on her stomach to give her back some color. The sand stirred around her, and she couldn't help thinking that this might be the end of the world—as if the giant hourglass that kept the time of the universe had shattered at its waist and spilled eternity here beneath her. The sand glittered like glass, confirming her suspicions, and she could feel its heat beneath her stomach like a child on a mother's chest.

The heat was the only good thing—the only thing she expected she'd miss. She wondered if the water would be warm when it flooded her lungs, warm enough to confuse her air sacks, maybe even warm enough to mingle into her blood through the linings. She liked salt, imagined it would be good to feel it coursing through her veins, if only for a moment. Regardless, she was sure it would taste good going down. It always had. In fact, that taste of sea water going places it shouldn't—up the nose and down the throat and slurping deep into the ears—was perhaps the only fond memory she had of her child-hood, swimming in the ocean with Daddy. Just the sense of invasion was fond—not Daddy himself. He taught her to swim by floating her on his knees. She could remember the scratchiness and the pokiness of his hairy thighs and chest coursing over her, a blanket of quills as he pulled her up out of the water whenever she sank too low, too long—wrestling wet with his body like a spiny fish with a long hard nose until surfacing to air, wind, his smiling face, his stale cigarette breath. She'd peek through the floating fabric of his shorts underwater during this training—seeing things she knew she shouldn't see—and Daddy always stayed in the water longer than she did allowing her to practice crawling back to the beach while he watched. He used to joke about evolution, but she never got it. By the time he came back to the beach where she and Mommy waited he always looked sunburned, but it never lasted long. It was really just blushing. Blushing while he finished a cigarette. Blushing while he avoided her eyes.

Some wind comes now—the sea air so salty she can almost feel the tiny crystals of salt pelting her eyelids, tiny pellets preparing her for the water, airborne particulates plugging her pores.

She thinks of Mommy, burying her in sand while they waited for Daddy. She'd always have a pit ready for her when she ran dripping and blowing snot from the edge of the water. Mommy liked playing with her toy shovel and bucket—Mommy always seemed jealous of her toys—and she would dig a hole in the sand while Daddy taught her to swim. It was a small hole usually, but it always reminded her of a grave. A grave she dove lovingly into—sometimes face-down—Mommy immediately shoveling sand on top of her as if to hide her from the sun's rays. They never spoke while they waited for Daddy. All she'd hear was the crunch of her bare stomach against water-soaked sand and the dull tap-tap-tap of the shovel above. Sometimes Mommy would use the plastic red shovel and bucket to build a sand castle on top of her—right on top of her tiny buried body—and it always looked as grand as a dollhouse. But Sandy didn't play with dolls—she liked to imagine that she was a giant who'd fallen asleep, only to find a house built right on top of her breasts while she slept. Mommy was an artist—she worked on clay pottery for a living. And she was good with sand. But no matter how good it was, she still felt like a zombie when she lifted herself out of Mommy's pretty grave. A huge zombie losing clumps of flesh—oh, okay, sand, but it sure did feel like skin when it peeled away to powder between her toes. Only no one paid any attention. No one was scared. Just quiet, like she wasn't even there.

So maybe today she would drown when no one was looking. And maybe—just maybe—that shark fisherman with the gray beard would notice her when she surfaced. Notice her—and do something about it. Maybe build her a house and bury her in the foundation. Maybe join her in the watery deep.

The wind was picking up. She buried her face in the towel, enjoying its sea bite. She could hear it whistling sharply through the waves—almost calling her name. Maybe it was the sound of people coming. Maybe a violent storm, instead. She didn't care. Shifting sand rustled around her, creating new dunes. Some sand tossed over her back, stinging the sunburned flesh like needle pricks. She let it settle on her, burn into her flesh like ashes from a campfire.

Death would be dust, sand, grit, but the water could wash that away. She'd rather be absorbed into nothingness—dilute her soul—than die dry. Even if it meant that her daydream fisherman would never find her.

The sand blew and whirled around her, sounding like she was

trapped inside a large ornate hourglass. Eyes clenched shut, she listened intently, waiting. Waiting. Waiting.

Soon the wind brought more sand into her ears, whirling inside the lobe like the grit in a gutted bone dry seashell. Its tiny rattling particles whispered to her. Mommy's voice: *you can drown in sand, too.* She tried to move but it was too late. She closed her eyes and listened in the silence for the pat-pat-pat of a plastic shovel, but knew when it finally came that it was only the final beats of a heart drying inside-out.

Holding her breath was no longer working. She tried to imagine a gray-bearded clam digger shoveling her free from the silt, but the image didn't work. It wasn't right; it wasn't what she had planned. So she tried to force the taste of salt on her tongue as she opened her mouth and let it in, fingering the wet gravel beneath her for Daddy's fingers, Daddy's kneecaps, anything bony to hold on to. There. There. Merely a cigarette butt. Fibrous and thick, deep in the wet sand, itchy against her thigh. Like buried treasure beneath Mommy's growing castle of salty sand. She fingered the rotting cylinder for a lingering warmth of lips, wondering if this is what plugged the waist of the universe's hourglass, causing it to explode and engulf her in sand like this as she hungrily writhed.

And swallowed.

Research Subjects

While I'm grading lab papers, a problem student in my bio class strolls into my office hours and drops down into a chair beside my desk.

"I'm losing it, Doc," he says, slapping an arm over his head to clutch the ear on the opposite side of it, looking something like a monkey. "I can't keep my shit together. And I don't know what to do."

I decide not to respond to his offensive cursing. I slowly set down my pen and look him in the eye. "Did you try researching the problem in the library yet?"

"No," he says and for a moment and I think I see a teardrop spill out of his right eye. "Just the internet."

"Well then..."

He turns away as if wincing in pain and I realize that droplet was no tear—it was a bright bead of blood, trickling down his cheek, spilling from a deep burgandy portion of matted blonde hair. He squeezes the monkey arm over his head more tightly and a plate in his skull audibly buckles.

"I know," he says with an exasperated huff and a roll of his good eye. "Go to the library."

"Yes," I say, returning to my paper. "Quickly. The deadline is looming."

"Thanks, Doc." He picks up his bag and moves toward my door.

"Oh, and Jimmy..."

"Yes?"

He turns around and I see a cluster of yellow matter on his shoulder, lumpy as grits. I wonder if his manners are in there, somewhere.

"Don't forget to knock next time." His eyes search the air, seeking the memory. "Now please shut the door."

He obeys. I lean back in the silence of my office and wonder how the rest of the class is doing with their experiments and whether or not I need to give more detailed directions next time.

NIGHTMARE JOB #5

You might have seen me on *Pet Patrol*. I'm the guy in the funky uniform who often accompanies the Humane Society enforcement agent when she batters down the doorway of a suspected pet hoarder. I'm the guy with the giant mitten and bite-guards who waits outside the door like some hockey goalie with a crazy assemblage of cages and nets. Waiting to collect the pet collector's pets.

Usually I'm off screen, though. What you don't see is that I'm the guy who captures the mangiest of the monsters—the ones so eager to escape from their own squalor that they've been clawing the fur clean off of their little paws, the muscles exposed like bloodied human fingers. They stain my uniform and soil my cages with their pus and drainage. They shiver in the back of my truck, shitting their innards, their brittle bones banging the cages. They're the real horror of the horror show; the stuff they never show you.

I can't help but think of the Holocaust when I release them into the dark chambers of my incinerator, where a ceramic bowl of fresh food waits, surrounded by the warmth of its tiles. Although the crematory machine's door is snug, I can still hear them scream in their ancient tongues while I spray their empty caddies clean with alcohol solvent. I cannot tell if their scream is one of joy or pain and this is what haunts me the most. I even hear them mewling softly in the back of my van as I return to the condemned home to harvest more of their kind.

I have grown accustomed to these ghosts over the years. Indeed: I've been hoarding them.

But I've only collected a few of their previous owners so far. Their cries, I ignore. I'm not ready to call them my pets quite yet.

How to Grow a
Man-Eating Plant

The secret to growing a man-eating plant is the same as it is with any plant: you must enrich the soil.

First, invest in blood meal. Not a five-pound sack from your local florist. Enough to fill half an oil drum. The other half will be filled with regular potting soil. Get the indoor/outdoor mix, because you'll want to grow this beast in private.

If blood meal isn't available, bone or meat meal will do the trick. But you want the blood meal if you can find it. It's got more protein. And it's the blood the man-eating plant wants as it develops. Not the meat. And certainly not the bones.

Regardless, you need to feed it from the get-go. As a seedling, the man-eating plant won't bite. You can safely use your hands to plant its evil seed in the soil. You'll want to place it deeper than most seedlings or bulbs. Go as deep as your elbow, at least. The deeper, the better. A good man-eating plant needs a deep root structure to anchor it in place when the man it's eating flails and fights for its life. So the deeper the seed, the stronger the root system. This is why you need so much blood meal. The man-eating plant doesn't care where it gets its blood. Whether in the hellish depths of earth or in the burning shine of the sun, it only thirsts—at this point—for blood protein.

Keep your drum in a warm, dark place and let it fester for several weeks. Keep away from it.

Most blood meal is composed of the waste derived from slaughter-houses. This does the trick to get the plant to sprout its spiky white roots during its fetal stages. But because it's not the blood of man, it deprives the plant of its core need for human nutrients. Therefore, *in utero*, the plant will grow chaotic and angry in the drum as it takes shape, laying down its foundation by thrusting its roots and feelers wantonly around the bloody soil until one stem manages to pierce the surface.

At this point several steps need to be taken.

First, you must provide a light source. The man-eating plant cannot grow further without the photosynthetic fuel of sunlight.

Next, you must provide a food source. The man-eating plant will wait no more. Blood meal will no longer do the trick. The young beastie now requires man meal.

Exercise caution. The man-eating plant does not have the capability of understanding the function of a keeper, feeder, guardian, gardener, collector, or parent. You will be its god, providing its sustenance, but the plant will not worship you. It will see you as food.

Since the plant is a child in want of a teat, it's useful to feed the plant children. They are easy to lure into the plant's reach. You don't even have to lie. Tell the child that you have a man-eating plant and curiosity will get the best of them. It does every time.

Don't worry about cleaning. The out of reach splatter will be an incentive for the plant to stretch its wiry frame to reach, just as a young philodendron will lean toward the window if grown indoors.

When the plant grows tall enough to actually eat a man with minimal harm, your job gets easier, not harder.

You can seduce scientists to visit your discovery. Or let the postal carrier in the door. Let the wife in on your secret project. It doesn't matter. Anyone will do.

But eventually, the man-eating plant will take over your life if you don't transplant it. And it's transplanting, not feeding, that's difficult.

You must provide so much food that the plant will become full. If satiated, the plant will not have the energy to eat you as you move its drum to a new location. However, it is virtually impossible to detect when a man-eating plant has had its fill of man meal. One trick is to shine a light at its stem and see if blood is actually apparent in its gullet. Another trick is to tease the creature with an extension of your own arm...like a dismembered limb that you hold from inside your sleeve as if it were your own hand. If the plant doesn't snap its large head onto the arm, you may safely move the plant.

But be sure not to take too long in transporting the man-eater. For they digest man meal quite quickly. It is recommended that you plant the creature as close as possible to its original location.

Most people will not recognize a man-eater even when they pass it by. You can safely plant the creature near a schoolyard or a library or even in a secluded alleyway. You need not worry about its meals seeing the plant coming. But you want to prevent others from witnessing the plant attacking its prey. So any place where people walk alone and in seclusion will do.

That doesn't mean that you can't see it in action, once in awhile, for old time's sake.

Send an arborist or a gardener to the scene. Bring your machete.

Even a healthy man-eating plant may occasionally need pruning. And remember: the older a plant gets, the more it needs a little help with its meal.

The Killer Descends

He walks into the elevator. An older woman backs away, giving him space, her eyes locked on the button board. He feels the survival knife in the puddly pocket of his trench coat. Its blade is still hot with murder. He stares at the woman and waits for her to dare to look at him. She doesn't. The doors swoosh shut and the elevator dings. He secretly hugs the flat of the metal against his thigh, caressing the steel, feeling the blood staining a bit through the pocket's waterproof fiber to greet his fingertips. He steals a glance at his shoes—blood droplets bead on the toes like unshined spit. The blade cools clammy in his pocket. The woman watches the countdown, oblivious. So does he as he sidles one step closer toward her, wondering just how much of her space he'll have to invade before she'll dare to give him her eyes.

Gasp

He posited that a person could drown in air. I told him to stop being contradictory. He raised a finger. Inhaled to reply. And never stopped.

DOMESTIC FOWL

I knew a man who transformed himself into a chicken over the course of two weeks.

He plucked his hair. Initially in bloody clumps, tearing them from his scalp like a cook threshes lettuce. Then tweezers for the rest. Each and every pore.

When I first saw his skin—his head only half-bald; his right arm only two-thirds hairless—I asked if he'd ever thought of using a razor.

"Chickens don't shave," he said, the little nub on his throat somehow giving him trouble. "And besides, I have to pluck." He was having difficulty swallowing. "I just have to. Because...because...be-gawwk!"

And that was the last time he used the English language.

I saw him again, a week later, in the supermarket. He had reached his goal. He was without hair. He was without hair and sitting Indian-style on the eggs in aisle three of the market. Yellow yolk spotted his naked thighs, which he had somehow pulled up under himself like a fleshy nest. He crossed his arms to hide his hands and puffed out his chest with a hen's pride. But occasionally, he would fidget and the Styrofoam egg cartons would squeak beneath his ass or the recycled gray cardboard ones would pop like dull bubble wrap.

Although his legs might as well have been shaved, he was clearly still male. I caught sight of his dangling masculinity when he rearranged his legs. I winced at the thought of those tweezers plucking down there; but from the pocks I'd seen, he'd clearly gone through with it. There were tiny divots of goose flesh everywhere, not just in his groin. But the sight of his crotch brought up a thought and so I asked him point blank: "Why a chicken, my man? Why not a rooster?"

"Be-gawwk!"

I guess that was his way of saying "Because...just because." To check his sanity, I asked him to hand me a gallon of milk. He obliged.

I dared not reach for a carton of Large Grade A's. He might have been a chicken boy, but he eyeballed me—and all the other patrons—with the daring stare of the hungry hawk. We were afraid he might peck us. After all, he'd somehow managed to break his face apart and reshape his nose and jaw into a skeletal beak. A real one. The skin peeled back pink at the base of it in a bloody cuticle.

I could only stare at him for so long before finishing up my shopping and heading home. As I stood in the Express Lane, the front doors of the market gasketed open and a battery of police came running inside. They barged through the register lanes against traffic, and they obviously meant business. I knew they were after my fowl friend.

I was about to shout a warning for him, but he was already running out the door, flapping his akimbo arms, several cartons of eggs clutched tightly against his chest. He was saving his children. Or at least the ones he hadn't crushed all runny with his legs when he first made his roost.

The last time I saw him, he actually came to my house. The bell rang and when I opened the door he was low on the stoop, pecking around. His transformation was nearly complete. His eyelids were gone. A protrusion appeared under his scalp where a hen's comb might be. His beak of bone had matured to full length. His stomach had bloated and his backside had swept impossibly upward into the full rotund shape of the chicken ass. The muscles in his arms had atrophied. The flesh dangled from the bone like an old person's—or more accurately, like a greasy pair of Buffalo wings at the local pub. Wings. Sadly, they were incapable of flight but he had miraculously grown them, nevertheless. There were no hands to speak of.

He hobbled around on two taloned feet, communicating with me by gesturing with quick snaps of his head. He'd peck the ground if he spotted something grain-like. But mostly, he nodded over and over again for me to follow him.

I obeyed. It took awhile for us to get where we were going because everything looks like food to a chicken.

Eventually, he led me to our destination: the backyard, where an ax had been plunged violently into the exposed trunk of a tree stump.

He jumped on the stump. Strutted like Mick Jagger.

"Why?" I pleaded, reluctantly yanking the ax free.

This time he just looked at me, his head cocked to one side.

Appendix A

On Writing Flash Fiction:

An Interview with Michael A. Arnzen
Conducted by Jerry Schatz for *FlashFictionFlash Newsletter*

Schatz: What do you like about flash fiction?

Arnzen: I like flash fiction that makes the most out of the brevity of the form—not long stories masquerading as short ones, but fiction that exploits the limitations of space. I've been writing a lot in the form lately as a personal challenge, really. I want to force myself to unlearn all the habits I've picked up from my training in other forms of writing. Writing flash regularly—sometimes several a day—has taught me how to edit myself more closely than I've ever been able to—and it's really got me in a new habit of getting the most juice out of verbs. I also am learning to really appreciate the art of indirect suggestion. I'm really proud of the stories I've written under 50 words that still "work." Those are hard as hell to pull off.

Schatz: What *is* flash fiction in your mind?

Arnzen: All flash fiction lovers should pick up a copy of *Sudden Stories*—an anthology from Mammoth Books (www.mammoth-books.com). For that book, editor Dinty Moore asked all the contributors to define "sudden stories" for possible use in the intro. I wrote back that I defined them as "efficiency narratives...an ice cube of plot whose theme thaws with time." That's how I usually conceive of them. Dense moments that stick with you.

Schatz: Why do you write it?

Arnzen: Although I've been publishing for a long time now, I was very skeptical about electronic publishing at first. Up until about two years ago, I was afraid of the ease of plagiarism through electronic means and I didn't think there was much of an audience for e-texts. But then I finally realized that e-publishing is just one market opportunity among many that are offered to writers, and with the rising affordability of handheld computers (e.g. e-book readers) and broadband internet, I saw the light. So I was determined to test the waters and I started with webzines. And the smarter webzines were publishing flash because they realize that people aren't patient enough (or even visually equipped) to read long pieces on screen. So flash fiction is ideal for the electronic marketplace. And the more I started writing it, the more I understood the experimental opportunities it afforded, much like poetry. The more I researched, the more I read, and the more I fell in love with flash. I discovered sites like *The-Phone-Book.com*, which were serving up mini-stories written in glyphs and code for cell phone delivery. I found *minima* magazine, who put their "small and potent" stories into ground-breaking "flash" animation. And by then I was completely won over.

Schatz: How about the print venues?

Arnzen: Although the reading practices on the internet seem custom-fit for flash fiction, the genre has a long history and a vibrant life in print, too. There's a magazine called *Quick Fiction* (jppress.org) which I subscribe to and admire quite a bit. It's a pocket-sized book filled with literary shorts. I also have a fondness for the small press magazines in the horror genre—*Wicked Hollow* (blindside.net) especially comes to mind—which celebrate short forms. There are classic books in flash which should be required reading for all writers—from the *Sudden Fiction* anthologies to Jerome Stern's *Micro Fiction* to Dinty Moore's *Sudden Stories*, which I already mentioned. And then there's classic prose-poetry. Baudelaire wrote prose poems which are worth studying too, as a birth of the genre, of sorts. And Kafka did a number of a parable-like pieces that I recall studying when I started writing seriously.

The economy of the fiction marketplace influences what we have to read. Because so many print magazines and books historically pay by the word, so many good writers go for longer stories and don't bother with short stuff. If more markets paid higher scales for shorter works (like *Vestal Review* and *flashquake* do) then maybe things would change. But because of the way fiction writing is presently reimbursed by word, there's less incentive for writers to try their hand at flash than there is with longer works. And that's why the web is an exciting place for flash—because the "new economy" on the internet is rewarding those who can write tightly. People who read on-screen don't want to scroll a lot, so longer stories just don't work well online. The form is influencing the market and the genre as a whole.

Schatz: Roughly speaking, about what percentage of your work is flash?

Arnzen: I'm not sure about percentages, but I'd say that I work on flash as often as I do anything else with writing. I have a long-range plan of compiling the best (and darkest) one hundred pieces I produce into a print collection entitled *100 Jolts*. I'm almost finished and a horror fiction publisher has already shown interest. But for me it's not just about publishing the book but producing something really original. And think about how much more you get for your money when you buy a book-length collection of a hundred short stories as opposed to the stock ten or twelve. I think my readers will like it.

Schatz: What are the major differences, to you, in writing flash or longer fiction?

Arnzen: Well, people assume flash is for short attention spans, but I don't think so at all. It's more like haiku.

Longer fiction spends more time with characters and settings. Flash fiction is just as interested in these things, but the plot is moving too fast for the writing to focus on them for very long. Or if it does, the details *are* the plot. There's very little difference, really, except with flash the emotions are condensed onto that "single desired effect" that Poe once spoke of as the goal of all short fiction. Sometimes flash fails because it lacks the character depth. But a skilled writer can imply a lifetime in a character's gesture. Of course, the reader is sometimes required to do more work. Just because flash fiction *looks* simpler doesn't mean it is. The good flash writers just make it look easy.

Schatz: So is writing flash harder or easier for you than writing longer fiction?

Arnzen: I think I write both equally well, but I find it easier to edit flash. One can get lost tracking down loose threads in a novel-length piece; if it's all on one page, it's remarkably easier to work with what's there and see the "big picture" at the same time. Though, of course, editing flash fiction offers its own difficulties. Like knowing when to *stop* cutting. Sometimes I find myself hacking out large chunks of what I've done in an effort to condense…and then I'm left with over-simplistic narrative or a vignette that implies too much, like a vacuous haiku poem. And because there are fewer words on the page, flash does require an extra close attention to diction and rhythm…luckily, I write poetry, too, which helps me in this department.

Despite many editorial guidelines or calls for clarity in workshops, many flash writers are writing prose-poetry and vignettes rather than narrative fiction. For me the distinction is rather moot; I think it's all poetic. But flash still has to "pay off" the way good fiction pays off. Conflict has to dominate the piece and spur the movement from plot point to plot point (and most flash pieces dramatize just one "plot point" and imply the weight of the rest). It doesn't require resolution, but a cagey ending that implies either closure or irony "cinches" a good flash piece and lets us feel like we've just read fiction. The structure of many flash pieces is the structure of the joke...and, purists be damned, that's fine! If a flash story is a joke structure masquerading behind rich evocative language, then it will likely pack a powerful punch. I'm not saying it has to generate a belly laugh, but, instead, catch us off guard and play off our expectations the way a really good joketeller can.

Flash can be really subversive that way. It's so deceptively simple. So "innocent" in its invitation to those with short attention spans to pay more attention!

Schatz: Do you write every day? Do you have a writing regimen you adhere to, or try to adhere to?

Arnzen: I try to write every morning for two hours, over the first cups of coffee. I'm a full-time writing teacher, though, so sometimes grading and preparations and other things get in the way. This is why I like flash: I don't feel like my whole day is required to draft and compose. I know before I ever start writing a flash that I can *probably* finish a good draft in one sitting and revise it later. Not always true. It's like "baby steps"—easier to climb a hill than a mountain. Sometimes teaching gets in the way, but I try to remind myself that my own writing is just as important as my students'.

There are also times when I'm not in the mood to write, and to be honest, I don't when my body and spirit tells me not to. But I still usually force myself to write daily because I know that if I start, the ideas will come and I'll get so immersed in the writing that I'll be productive. It's like diving into a pool—once you're in, you swim. So trying to write every day in the morning is kind of like diving into the pool and seeing what happens. I never get writer's block. But I do get language burn-out. Editors reading this can empathize—too much reading of other people's words, too much critiquing and editing and talking kind of wrings out the sponge. So there are times when I dive into that "pool" I was talking about, but there are too many other people in there, swimming around, and I get distracted.

Schatz: Where do you find inspiration for your writing?

Arnzen: In the reader. It's that simple. I don't try to come up with ideas; they come to me and I feel like it's my duty to deliver them to the reader well. I find them at the bottom of that pool I was talking about before. Dive in and it's there. The well hasn't run dry yet. I know that as long as I can surprise myself, I can surprise my reader, and so writing—especially horror writing—is like a constant search in the murky unknown on a quest to be surprised. I do outline or plot out ideas sometimes, but I let the story take charge once I've started writing and edit it later.

Schatz: What are your thoughts on online critiquing groups?

Arnzen: Editors and writers used to have a teacher-student relationship; the writer is like an apprentice to the craft, under the editor. I don't think that's the case so much anymore, because the competition is so fierce for publishing spots that editors expect writers to be full-blown pros when they get them. So writers need to share their experiences and bounce ideas off each other to really learn to develop those skills that editors are expecting you to have.

Although some would disagree with me, I think formal educational programs are still the best. You're likely to get an experienced professional as your guide and many writing workshops that are attached to schools do incorporate an online component these days. At Seton Hill University, where I teach, we offer a combination of "intensive residency" with distance learning so our Master's students get the best of both worlds. Learning doesn't necessarily have to come through a degree program however (though I would say that there you'll be likely to get the most practiced "teachers"). Community workshops, writer's retreats and genre conventions can really open your eyes to the business quite a bit. Online critique groups can help a lot, too. The more formal, the better, I think—otherwise you risk the blind leading the blind. I like the model that Zoetrope Studios (zoetrope.com) has instituted, which enforces collaborative learning—you have to critique five stories before you can post your own for workshopping by others. I understand the

FlashFiction-W workshop listed in this newsletter has a similar requirement. Others are lead by pros that require some form of payment to enroll...those can be useful too, if the leader or moderator knows what they're doing and is not just good at writing, but also good at teaching with technology. I've heard nothing but good things about Pamelyn Casto's flash fiction workshops, for example. Overall, the internet is often compared to a library—and in a way, the whole web can become the "textbook" of an online course. Good programs will produce good writers who will keep authoring that book well into the future.

Schatz: How important *is* formal training in creative writing?

Arnzen: It's not crucial, but it's very useful. You can make connections and network with folks you'd never meet otherwise. Learn shortcuts. Relearn the basics. Cultivate the writer's mind. Find out what to read. Get feedback without the painful and slow process of getting it from editors. And—most importantly—you can find a community of like-minded spirits and connect to a history of others who are just like you. I recommend it to all writers, if only just one class or one online workshop. Writing can be such a lonely, alienating business that schooling really helps to make it real and make it social. I teach in a graduate program for Writing Popular Fiction at Seton Hill University. People from all genres come together to critique each other and study together under the tutelage of published novelists. Everyone learns a lot. But most people leave the program with friends for life. People who they can "talk writing" with and swap stories and pat each other on the back. That's more important than any printed publication—be it a book, a story...or even a diploma.

And I should add that I've been using selected fifty-word fictions to teach writing strategies in the program, too. That's how much I believe in the genre. Good flash fiction distills good fiction to its essence and every writer can learn a lot from one simple tiny story.

Jerry Schatz is a published humorist and author of flash fiction. His work has appeared in *The Green Tricycle* and *Laughter Loaf* and *Muse Apprentice Guild*. He lives in King of Prussia, PA, and is a contributing writer for *FlashFictionFlash* newsletter. Schatz can be reached at: jerry.schatz@verizon.net

Appendix B

Acknowledgments

About half of the stories in this collection have been published in various magazines, anthologies, and online venues. I want to acknowledge the hard work of the editors of each of these publications and commend them on their dedication to the short form. (I also want to thank John Edward Lawson, Jennifer C. Barnes, and Vincent W. Sakowski for bringing their keen editorial eyes and wisdom to the pages of this book. Extra thanks go to Matt Sesow, Renate Arnzen, and Jerry Schatz.)

"Beyond Undead" first appeared in *FlashShot*, Dec 2002.

"Brain Candy" first appeared in *FlashShot*, Jan 2004.

"The Blood Ran Out" first appeared in *100 Vicious Little Vampire Stories*, 1995.

"Burning Bridges" first appeared in *The Murder Hole*, Jun 2002.

"Canines" first appeared in *FlashShot*, Nov 2002.

"A Change in Policy" first appeared in *Needles and Sins*, 1993.

"Choppers" first appeared in *42opus*, Dec 2002.

"Contused" first appeared in *FlashShot*, Mar 2003.

"Convictions" first appeared in *Worlds of Surrealism*, Winter 1990.

"Crusty Old Age" first appeared in *The Goreletter*, Oct 2002.

"The Curse of Fat Face" first appeared in *Vestal Review*, Oct 2002.

"Disgruntled" first appeared in *The Murder Hole*, Mar 2003.

"A Donation" first appeared in *Zoiks!*, 1989.

"Face of Clay" first appeared in *FlashShot*, Oct 2002.

"Gasp" first appeared in *FlashShot*, Nov 2002.

"Her Daily Bread" first appeared in *The Eternal Night*, May 2003.

"How to Grow a Man-Eating Plant" first appeared in *The Eternal Night*, Jun 2003.

"How to Put a Cat to Sleep" first appeared in *Literary Potpourri*, Jul 2003.

"In the Middle" first appeared in *Insolent Rudder*, Sept 2002.

"Inside the Man with No Eyelids" first appeared in *Black Lotus*, Fall 1993.

"Introduction: Minimalist Horror" first appeared on *gorelets.com*, Dec 2002 (under the title, "Knife Wounds").

"Jack the Teacher" first appeared in *Alien Skin*, May 2003.

"Knock Off the Auction Block" first appeared in *FlashShot*, May 2003.

"Latex" first appeared in *Fifty-Word Fictions*, Apr 2002.

"Limber" first appeared in *Alien Skin*, Apr 2003.

"Little Stocking Stuffers" first appeared in *FlashShot*, Dec 2002.

"Mortichinery" first appeared in *HorrorFind Fiction*, Aug 2002.

"Mother's Haunted Housecoat" first appeared in *Cemetery Poets: Grave Offerings*, 2003.

"Mustachio Moon" first appeared in *Dark Animus*, Mar/Apr 2003.

"My Wound Still Weeps" first appeared in *Horrors: 365 Scary Stories*, 1998.

"Next-Door" first appeared in *Tense Moments*, May 1991.

"Obictionary" first appeared in *EOTU*, Feb 2003.

"Phrenological Love" first appeared in *SPWAO Showcase*, 1992.

"Punishment" first appeared in *Champagne Shivers*, Jul 2002.

"Receiver" first appeared in *Detective Story Magazine*, Dec 1989.

"Research Subjects" first appeared in *Flash Fantastic*, 2004.

"Revenge of the Mummy" first appeared in *FlashShot*, Nov 2002.

"Second Helping" first appeared in *Of Flesh and Hunger*, 2003.

"The Seven-Headed Beast" first appeared in *Cemetery Poets: Grave Offerings*, Jan 2003.

"Sinking Sandy" first appeared in *Fugue*, Winter 1995.

"Skull Fragments" first appeared on *gorelets.com*, Aug 2003.

"Stomachine" first appeared in *Champagne Shivers*, Feb 2003.

"Strange Trout" first appeared in *The Goreletter*, Aug 2003.

"Stretch" first appeared in *A Bowl of Stories*, 2002.

"Surgical Complications" first appeared in *FlashShot*, Jan 2003.

"Take Out" first appeared in *minima*, Jul 2002.

"Taking Care of Baby" first appeared in *Raven Electrick*, Jul 2002.

"Trimachine" first appeared in *Flash Me*, Aug 2003.

"Tugging the Heartstrings" first appeared in *flashquake*, Winter 2002.

"Valendine" first appeared in *The Goreletter*, Feb 2003.

"White Out" first appeared in *Cemetery Poets: Grave Offerings*, Jan 2003.

"Who Wants to be a Killionaire?" first appeared in *HorrorFind Fiction*, Jul 2002.

"A Worse Mousetrap" first appeared in *ShadowKeep*, Jul 2002.

About the Author

Michael A. Arnzen is the author of the Bram Stoker Award-winning novel, *Grave Markings* (Dell Books). His short story collection, *Fluid Mosaic* (Wildside Press) collects his best stories from the 1990s. His poetry chapbooks include *Freakcidents*, *Gorelets: Unpleasant Poetry, Dying (With No Apologies to Martha Stewart), Paratabloids, Chew, Sportuary* and *Writhing in Darkness.*

Arnzen holds a Ph.D. in English and presently teaches graduate studies in "Writing Popular Fiction" at Seton Hill University in Western Pennsylvania, where he lives with his wife, Renate, and a brood of cats. He maintains a popular horror website at http://www.gorelets.com and publishes a free monthly newsletter of offbeat thought, *The Goreletter.*

Breinigsville, PA USA
21 February 2010
232887BV00001B/83/A